Grandad's stories

The Secret Coin

by Freddie Woodcock.

Honeybee
Books

Published by Honeybee Books
Broadoak, Dorset
www.honeybeebooks.co.uk

Printed in the UK using paper from sustainable sources

ISBN: 978-1-910616-28-4

Dedicated to my three grandchildren,
Jay Woodcock, Izabella Woodcock and Beau Watson.

I hope in some way this will inspire you to use your imagination in all you do.

Poem By Grandad Freddie

Send me high into the bluest sky,
When I look back I'll wave goodbye.
Stars crisp and white with their gentle light,
I'll guide you home on a winter's night.

17th of October 2013

Acknowledgements

Thanks go to my wife Debbie for her endless enthusiasm, my eldest son Jason for his persistence in fixing countless computer glitches, my youngest son Justin for his patience through hours of proofreading and my daughter Aloma for her kind and sincere words.

I would also like to thank my nephew Rob Steele for his brilliant Illustrations.

From the darkest of places to the modern world, technology is here to help you to find your freedom and express yourself. I've suffered with dyslexia all my life and I have used electronic software to help produce this book, so a big thanks to the electronic wizards of the world.

Don't be afraid of dyslexia, use all the tools you need.

Thank you for purchasing my first book; although a little late to start writing, at the age of 67, I do feel inspired to carry on.

Freddie

My father (or Pops as we call him) is one of those people who just simply makes the world a better place to be.

As one of seven, he was raised by his Maltese mother and English father in Birmingham. This shaped this all round gentleman into becoming the father to Jason, Justin and myself Aloma, and grandfather to Jay, Izzy and Beau, and the man that he is today.

Although coming from simple beginnings, where times were hard and money scant, my grandparents taught my father and his siblings to love unconditionally, to respect all no matter what religion or background, to support one another through all aspects of life and to always take pride in their appearance. Being a Woodcock is something all family members were very proud of and still are today, myself included. The time my dad spent with his father cultivated a love for both craftsmanship and the great outdoors that has stayed with him throughout his life. Time spent with his mum gave him the bug for cooking and entertaining, a lot, of which he still does today.

As a young boy, school became a problem for Pops as dyslexia was difficult to diagnose and hard to identify within such a large family, but with hard work and determination he's gone on to live as good a life as he can and not let this hurdle stand in the way of writing this children's book you are about to read. Writing is his latest passion in life along with many others: sailing, music (through which he met his amazingly supportive wife Debbie), nature, politics and socializing with his family and friends, are what complete this inspirational man.

It surprises me little that he would write a book for children. ALL children who are lucky enough to meet him love Freddie Woodcock. The father, grandfather, husband and brother who is renowned for his magic tricks, his jokes (occasionally forgetting the punchline) and his love for just "having the crack", putting a smile on everyone's face as he does so, makes him the man you just always want to be around whatever your age. I'm in my mid-thirties, my brothers are both in their early forties and we still giggle like small children whenever we are with him.

In a nutshell, this man (my father), his lifetime of dedication and self-sacrifice after raising my two brothers on his own, serves as a monument to the exemplary man he is.

His humility, integrity, hard work, sense of humor and love for life continue to inspire those who know him.

Chapter 1
A Cold Start

Tom gave the front door a gentle nudge before turning the key. It's a habit he'd gotten into some eighteen months earlier after losing all his possessions to opportunist thieves.

Turning to face down South Street, Tom zipped his coat, adjusted his scarf and gloves, then made his way into town, asking himself why he'd left the warmth of his bed on such a cold morning. The vibration on his leg went unnoticed until his phone began playing the first eight bars of his favorite song. Rushing to retrieve it he pressed the accept button before realizing who the caller was.

"How did you get my number?" demanded Tom.

"It's Dad here."

"I can see that! There's a problem or you're in need of something? Why else would you be bothering to track me down?" asked Tom.

"Now there's no need for that sort of talk, son. Yes, I need a favour."

"Oh I know you do. With your favours in the past with mum, they usually involve time or money, which one is it on this occasion?"

"Time is all I'm asking for, you'll benefit from the time you give but I need it now, son."

"Well there's a first, when have I ever received any benefits from you? When was the last time you tried to contact with me! How many years ago?

"I have my reasons."

"No. You had excuses."

"No, they weren't excuses. When your mother and I broke up I had to move away and get my life sorted out."

"Yeah, yeah, same old story, in fact I think I've heard enough!" Tom shouted down the phone.

Chapter 2
Life of Crime

Unknown to Tom, most of his father's childhood had been spent in care homes around the country. From the age of seven, Robin was known to the local police force after committing a series of small crimes. By the age of ten his criminal activities had become more serious. The courts had no other choice but to recommended he spent some time away from home in a children's correction centre, in the hope that Robin would retune to a normal life. On his sixteenth birthday, Robin was released and intended to leave his criminal activities behind, which he did for the next twenty-two years – until a so-called friend Howard Bloom offered Robin a chance to take part in a raid at a local garage.

It goes without saying that Robin's biggest downfall was due to his snap decisions. Rarely did he think things through before getting involved, which often left him with little or no way out of a bad situation. He'd fallen on hard times and desperately needed some ready cash. Again, without thinking and not worrying about the consequences, he took the bait, unaware that his friend would be carrying a gun and had every intention of using it should the need arise.

Inside the garage an elderly lady struggled with her coat as she made her way to the exit. Robin casually opened the door and bid her good morning, Howard waited until the coast was clear. Moving forward, he pointed the gun at the cashier and began to demand money.

"I haven't any money!" explained the cashier. "Mr Singh the owner hasn't arrived yet, so you've made a slight error, I'm thinking. Mr Singh has all the cash for the tills, that old lady and me are just the cleaners."

Howard became angry and raised the gun towards the cashier's chest. "I haven't got time for this, open the till!" he demanded.

"You can put that away, or I'll walk!" Robin shouted. For a brief moment Howard stood there, unsure what to do next.

"That's it, I'm out of here!" shouted Robin as he snatched a few items from the shelves.

The quick thinking cashier pressed the alarm button.

Howard looked up and noticed the CCTV camera, in his panic he tripped over a box on the floor and accidently fired his gun; a fine sticky mist of different colours filled the air as the bullet hit the display cabinet containing cans of fizzy drinks. Howard made his escape and left empty handed.

A few days later they stood in front of a very stern-faced judge and were about to pay a high price for their actions. Because Howard had threatened the casher with the gun, the judge increased his sentence from fifteen to twenty years, with no remission.

It was agreed that Robin had no prior knowledge of the firearm and taking this into account the judge said, "Whether you were, or were not aware that Mr Howard was carrying a firearm is not significant. You still took part in this criminal activity and must pay the price. This is why I'm sentencing you today to a long sentence as a deterrent to others that may follow in the future; I give you ten years which may be reduced on good behaviour." As the judge closed the files he looked over to Robin and said, "That, young man, depends solely on you!"

At the time of his release, Robin had reached the age of forty-eight.

Chapter 3
Freedom

Billy had known Robin since primary school, not as close friend, just someone he'd meet from time to time. Billy had heard through the grapevine that Robin was coming out of prison so decided to meet him outside the prison gate. In a local bar they talked about the old school days and how they'd changed.

Don't get me wrong," said Robin, "I'm grateful to have somebody meet me today, but why you?"

Billy explained that he'd heard about Robin's past and how he had been used in the garage raid, and that he was looking for someone who he could trust. "I'm offering you a chance of making a lot of money without breaking any laws; I believe we're all entitled to a second chance in life. This is yours, if you want it, Robin. I know you haven't been much of a friend of mine but that's my fault, I generally like to keep myself to myself, but I've realised I can't do this on my own."

"Do what?" asked Robin.

Billy continued for the next twenty-five minutes. When he'd finished he gave Robin time to think it over.

"Well," asked Billy, "you said you need me and maybe two more?"

"That's right."

"Can my son be one of the others?"

"Your son ever visited you in prison?" Billy asked.

"No," replied Robin.

"Then the answer's no, any son not standing by his dad in good and bad times ain't worth a monkey's fart."

"Look, I don't blame him, what I did was wrong. No wonder he didn't want anything to do with me. If he's not in then you can count me out, he's a good kid, Billy. He won't let us down, it's my chance to show him I'm not all bad."

Billy gave Robin a hard stare as he thought it over. "Well OK, I'll go along with this but any problems, you sort them out between you and your son. Don't let it interfere with our project, agreed?"

"Agreed," said Robin.

Chapter 4
An Old Friend

That's when the search for Tom began. After months of searching following good and bad leads in all sorts of weather Robin was handed a phone number for one of Tom's old friends, Phil Azzopardi. The line seemed dead at first but Robin was sure he'd heard something in the background, he held his breath hoping to catch what was being said on the other end of the line but the sound was too distant.

"If anyone's there please pick up, please," Robin shouted. Then he heard someone's voice on the other end.

"Hey man, what's your grass, brother?"

"Phil! Is that you? It's Robin, Tom Slater's father."

"Who you say?"

"It's Tom's father, I'm trying to get hold of Tom's new number. We lived next door to you some years ago, when you were just kids, remember?"

"I ain't remembering that far back, ain't good for the brain cells man."

"OK Phil," said Robin, "Let me remind you of a few thing to jog your memory." A few minutes went by.

"Hey man, ain't you the daddy that left him?"

Not quite the response Robin was hoping for. The tone in Robin's voice dropped, "Yeah that's me."

"Then I ain't passing on anything to you man!"

Robin had to think quickly and did what he always did in situations like this and came up with a story.

"Hang on Phil, let me explain why I'm calling then decide whether you pass on Tom's number."

"I'm listening."

"OK. Tom's auntie Grace passed away a few days ago and left Tom some money,"

"Well that ain't yours man."

"No I realize that, she'd always hoped that one day Tom and I would get back together so she's put it in her will. If Tom were to receive his inheritance we'd have to go together. I suppose it's her way of making sure we meet up, even if it's just for one day. It's the only way Tom would get his money; I'm sure as his mate, you wouldn't want to prevent him from getting what he's entitled to."

"No man! I ain't like that, whilst you been a talking I've been a looking and searching and come across diss information. You just tell him one thing man, tell him I gives you the number, he might send me a couple of quid you know! You do that?" Robin agreed.

After being shouted at down the phone, Robin realized the difficulty he would have trying to convince Tom that he was going straight and life was about to change for the better.

"Tom, don't walk away from this please don't walk away from something that may bring us closer together. It may not, but one thing's for sure, son, if this works out, your money worries are over. I owe you this, please let me do this one thing, if it doesn't work out forget me. I promise I'll never contact you again; you have my word on that."

What does he know about honesty and keeping his word, Tom thought as he focused on the urgency in his father's voice.

The line went quiet for a while. "OK," said Tom, "where and for how long?"

"It's not as straightforward as that,"

"It never is."

"Look, we need to meet and discuss the course of action," said Robin.

"If this is some kind of a con to get us sitting round the table so you can harp on about the past, you're wasting your time." Tom's comments didn't register at all.

"Let's meet at Franklin's bar at 8:30 p.m. Friday evening," suggested Robin.

"OK 8:30 it is," Tom replied and finished the call.

Chapter 5
The Big Man

Pushing the door open, Tom felt the warm air against his face as he entered the Internet café, requesting his usual coffee with nod of the head. Since moving back into his hometown, Tom had made this is regular meeting place three times a week for his morning coffee and a chance to read the free local newspaper. Unusually busy for a Tuesday morning, Tom thought as he squeezed through the overcrowded and somewhat noisy room to a vacant table. His body temperature soon began to rise but his fingertips remained cold, after removing his scarf and jacket he pulled out a chair and gave his hands a gentle rub as he sat down. Graham, the café manager, placed the coffee and a newspaper on the table. "Good morning to you Tom on this bright but nippy autumn morning."

"Morning," Tom replied, as he gently placed his hands around the hot mug. "Good trade this morning, Graham, where's everybody come from?" Tom asked.

"I believe they're doing something in Roll Street, no doubt digging up the same holes they dug up a fortnight ago. Still, it's good for business so I'm not complaining," Graham replied with a slight grin on his face. "Would there be anything else, Tom?" he asked.

Tom looked up in the direction of the jingling doorbell and raised his hand to acknowledge his new friend Paul.

"What can I get you?" Graham asked.

"Coffee for starters please. You having breakfast, mate?" enquired Paul.

"No, I'm a bit short of readies at the moment," replied Tom.

"No worries, mate. I've just been to the bank so the grub's on me." Pausing, Paul sensed Tom's embarrassment and ordered two full English breakfasts.

"Would you like bread and butter or toast with that," Graham asked. They both agreed on toast.

"Top up that coffee?" Graham suggested pointing to Tom's half-empty mug.

"Yes sure," replied Paul.

Left alone they began to catch up on the week's events. They were both keen Chelsea supporters and were more than pleased with their 3–2 win against Stoke, but sorry to hear that yet again another pitch invasion had taken place. This time it was at Aston Villa in Birmingham, all because the referee had sent off a player for a dangerous tackle. They both agreed that if this type of behaviour continued it would discourage families from going to the game, and it was about time the FA got it sorted once and for all.

"So how is the job hunting going?" Paul enquired, raising his voice as a loud cheer went up from the opposite table. It looked like one of the road crew; a big burly bloke with a black beard and weighing about twenty-eight stone had become the target of all the jokes. Feeling safe in their numbers the rest of the pack took what must've been a rare opportunity to gang up on him. But it was obvious to Tom that nobody wanted to be caught laughing last. The big man wasn't laughing, he just nodded his head and blushed slightly.

"Absolutely nothing, mate," replied Tom looking back at Paul. "I've already applied for several jobs this week, I don't care what anybody says about there being nothing out there, it's a joke. I want work and I'm willing to do anything. I'm sick and fed up of having no money in my pocket, lots of time to waste but no money to enjoy it. Two years ago, mate, I had a nice car, girlfriend and plenty of money, today I've got nothing." Tom looked up. "Sorry mate, sorry to burden you with all my troubles."

"Hey, that's what friends are for," said Paul as their breakfasts arrived.

"There you go, boys. Enjoy, but remember, any complaints and you keep them to yourselves."

"Thanks, Graham. On top of that," Tom re-engaged, "I've had a phone call from the old man, totally unexpected. You know I haven't seen or heard of him for years, and when I do it's a demand of some sort or other."

"What type of demand?" asked Paul.

"He wants to meet me at Franklins, he's going on about making a fortune and wants me involved – all legal and above board of course! Or so he says. I can hardly remember what he looks like."

"Yeah but there's an offer you can't refuse, I know you don't see him much, but you're going along aren't you? What caused the bad feelings between you and your dad anyway?" asked Paul.

Tom gave Paul a hard stare, enough for Paul to realize he'd overstepped the mark. Quickly changing the subject. Paul informed Tom that he too would be joining the dole queue in the next few weeks. Reluctantly Tom asked why.

"Apparently, as I'm the last one in the company I have to be the first to leave."

"I understand that," said Tom. "But surely there's someone willing to take early retirement so a younger person can have a future to look forward too?"

"I know what you mean, but it doesn't work like that anymore, everybody's looking after themselves these days, both young and old."

"Well, it doesn't seem right to me, but at least with your qualifications you shouldn't be out of work for too long!"

"I'm not sure about that, most of the so-called 'white collar' workers are getting laid off this time round."

Graham approached the table. "Can I get you anything else, lads?"

"No thanks, my parking ticket is about to run out."

"How about you Tom?"

"I'm on my way too, thanks Graham."

As they squeezed past the other diners, Tom attempted to put his arm through the sleeve of his jacket and lost his balance. As he did so, he fell against the big guy. A loud cheer filled the air as a hot mug of tea landed in the big guy's lap. Tom had no chance to react; the big guy stood up, taking Tom by the scruff of his neck, forcing him on the table.

He tried to say sorry but the big guy was pressing hard against his windpipe. Paul and Graham tried to pull him off but he was too strong for them, Tom's face began to turn blue. Thankfully a member of the road crew decided to intervene. "Leave the boys alone," he shouted as he delivered a daring right-hook to the big man's jaw.

Silence fell; the big man stood still for a while and loosened his grip from around Tom's neck then looked around the room. He'd understood why he'd received such a blow and quietly made his way to the front door. Looking back over his shoulder he mouthed to Tom. "I'll catch up with you some other time." Graham read his lips,

"Well that won't be here, you can take your custom elsewhere," Graham shouted. The door slammed, almost shattering the glass and set off the alarm, the rest of the road crew picked up their personal belongings and made a quiet exit.

"You all right, Tom?" asked Graham.

"Yeah no worries, all the jokes have been aimed at him this morning, I suppose me bumping into him was the final straw."

"Nevertheless mate," said Paul, "that's out of order, I wonder if he'd do the same to someone his own size?"

Outside the café Paul apologized for asking too many questions regarding Tom's father.

"It's OK, mate," said Tom. "When the time is right I'll explain."

Chapter 6
Moving Home

Stewart Redgrave had worked for the Forestry Commission just outside Birmingham for the last twelve years. Starting as a yard hand he quickly rose through the ranks, finally ending up as a manager. The company offered good wages, a yearly bonus, a good pension scheme and a friendly working environment. There hadn't been any vacancies at the Birmingham branch for the last six years and Stewart used this as his personal indicator to show how well he'd been doing as manager, keeping everybody focused and happy, which wasn't without its problems at times.

Sitting at his desk he began going through his paperwork and came across the company's monthly magazine. Skip reading until he reached page nine and the company's vacancies, he read on the top left hand corner 'It is with regret we announce the loss of Ken Bleakly. Ken passed away peacefully last month… he was an outstanding and loyal senior manager for the last fifteen years and will be sorely missed by all. Our thoughts and condolences go to his immediate family'. On the opposite page, Stewart was surprised to see the post being advertised and felt it a bit premature. It stated that interested parties should apply within three working weeks and that any applications received after 25th February 2011 would not be accepted. Only managerial staff needed apply.

This position would normally be offered to an under-manager before going out to the rest of the managerial staff, so this could only mean one of two things, Stewart thought. Either the under-manager didn't want the position, or he wasn't up to the job.

At home, Stewart waited until the children had gone to bed and Jane was ready to settle down for the evening. As he entered the living room carrying a bottle of her favourite wine Montepulciano, Jane asked, "What's the big occasion?"

"There's a vacancy at the Cornish depot, one of the biggest in the country."

"Cornwall sounds very nice," said Jane reaching for a glass.

Stewart placed the tray on the small swivel table attached to his armchair, he knew he would have a hard job convincing Jane to move away from her parents but he had to give it a try. Stewart began his sales pitch. "With this position, sweetheart, comes a four-bedroom house – one of the biggest in the group – sitting on a ten acre site right on the coast."

Jane sipped her wine.

"Imagine having all that land with glorious views out to sea, the children would be able to make as much noise as they liked and the dogs would have the run of the place. It sounds too good to be true." After a slight pause she added, "Go on then, what's the salary?" Stewart quickly brought Jane up to date with all the details.

"It must be the highest paid position in the company!"

"Well one of them."

"Why so?"

"It's the isolation, as a senior manager you're on your own with sole responsibility of twenty-five employees."

More silence, a chance to think things over, Stewart thought.

"It's a wonderful opportunity for someone," said Jane breaking the silence. "I bet every man and his dog will apply."

"Yes they probably will," Stewart said quietly. "Look, Jane, I was thinking of applying myself, obviously we need to talk things over first."

"Do you really think they'd consider you for this post? I mean you've only been a manager for a short time."

"Yes that's true, Jane, but in my 'short time' as you put it, I've shown I'm prepared to take on all sorts of responsibilities, look how I've progressed in a relatively short time, surely that's an advantage." Stewart was in full flight. "I get on well with everybody, get the job done and I'm ready to take on more responsibilities. Yes, I have a few concerns; moving house finding the right school for the children, a school that offers as many opportunities both in education and sports as Claybrook does. The children will need to make new friends, but I feel it's right, Jane – not just for me but all of us, it's worth applying for. This could be the chance we've be waiting for, so why let someone else take it away from us without a fight?"

Like all working mothers, Jane had many roles, running the family home, working as a part-time secretary and occasionally waitressing at her friend's wine bar. The last few years had taken their toll.

She felt trapped, unhappy with the way her working life had taken over and felt guilty she wasn't spending enough time with the children, at times it seemed almost impossible just to stop and catch her breath. Yes, this increased salary would give her the opportunity to give up work, it's what Jane wanted with her first child, Jay, but they couldn't afford it at the time, that opportunity was here now.

"What do you think?" Stewart asked.

"My word, you have been giving this some thought, that was some sales pitch," said Jane reaching for the wine. "It's a big change for the children and you know how much they love their school and how well they're doing. Jay won't be pleased if it means giving up his football, there's not a lot of young lads who get a chance to play for the shadow squad at West Bromwich Albion Academy. His sports cover such a wide range from football to cricket, swimming, basketball, netball, kickboxing, running – the list goes on and on, sports are a big part of his life. Look at Izabella, academically she's flying, you know how much she loves her horse riding, so the only way you'll get Izabella to move is on the promise that one day she'll have her own horse."

"Well that can be arranged," Stewart interrupted.

"Gymnastics," Jane continued, "look how well she's doing. She swims for the school now and that means a lot to her, then there's the dancing school with all the friends. What about Beau? Academically he's doing really well, another outdoor fanatic, never missing a game of rugby, he could well become a sailing instructor at the local club and his martial arts has impressed everyone. Almost everything I've just mentioned, Stewart, is either within the school or nearby, so finding a school like Claybrook won't be easy." Stewart knew Jane was right and sat quiet for quite some time. Sensing Stewart's disappointment Jane asked when the applications had to be in by.

"Seriously?!" said Jane. "They expect us to make our minds up within three weeks? They must be mad."

"I know there's a lot to discuss and three weeks doesn't seem long for such a monumental decision, but that's all the time we have. I say fill in the application, it will take them a few months to process them all. Am I being over ambitious? I don't know! If I did get the job it would take them six months before they put me in place, you know how slow the company works."

Jane thought it over. "OK, I'll go along with this, but don't be too disappointed, Stewart, if you don't get it."

"And what if I do?"

"Let's just wait and see what happens."

A few days later the children had the opportunity to have their say and surprised their parents by their reactions. Jay informed his parents that although Cornwall didn't have a football league club they had produced players like Nigel Martyn and Matthew Etherington and both had represented England at various ages and he could still carry on with his football career if he wanted to. Izabella, straight to the point as ever, said that as long as she had a horse she couldn't see a problem with moving. Beau knew there was lots of rugby clubs in Cornwall and liked the idea of being closer to the Cornish Pirates rugby squad. All three children agreed it would be nice to have Mum at home and welcomed the idea of a fresh start and a new adventure.

Weeks flashed by discussing the pros and cons. They managed to find a private school for borders and non-boarders, with good academic and brilliant sporting facilities that wouldn't be too far from their new home. Mr Greaves, the school's headmaster, had read the children's reports and sent a letter back a few days later, saying they would welcome all three as non-boarders. The children's excitement reached fever pitch. All they had to do now was to wait and see if Stewart had got the job.

Chapter 7
The Interview

Five weeks later and Stewart was summoned to the head office in Lutterworth, Leicestershire. On his arrival Mr Yardley's very efficient, but unfriendly, secretary showed Stewart into the main office and pointed to an upright leather chair, she waited until Stewart had taken his seat then left the room without a word. Mr Yardley sat behind a huge oak table sucking on a cigar whilst going through some papers. Stewart sat looking at family portraits and aerial photographs of all the forests throughout the United Kingdom, on the back wall and in pride of place stood a very impressive display cabinet, not trophies but of whiskey from around the world. As a whiskey drinker Stewart strained his eyes trying to read the labels,

either they were too small or too far away. Eventually, Mr Yardley looked over the rim of his glasses and took Stewart by surprise.

"There you are," he shouted. "Congratulations, Stewart!" Before Stewart had a chance to say thank you, Mr Yardley continued, "Now look here, we need to discuss the finer details of the job, salary, bonuses that sort of thing, your only contact with head office will be by landline until we establish a better communication with that new inter-netting thing." Without taking a single breath, Mr Yardley continued, "I've been told mobile phones don't work in or around the forest so not much point in purchasing any of those either. Did I tell you that? Did I? Oh well there it is, ah yes, your salary will increase from £47,000 to £75,000 per annum.

"Now, of course you get that beautiful house, used it myself many years ago. And, oh yes, one of the new forestry vehicles, well that's enough of that. Let's have a drink to celebrate your success," said Mr Yardley. Stewart couldn't help thinking how matter of fact Mr Yardley had become.

"Well," Mr Yardley continued. "I hope you find the job both satisfying and challenging." Then he looked down at the papers on his desk. Stewart was about to say something in agreement, but was interrupted once more. "I see from our records you have many talents! Now, what impressed me, young man, and the reason why you're standing here today is your knack of finding and maintaining a decent workforce, gaining trust and respect is commendable and paramount to the future of this company." Stewart was about to say I agree. "Oh yes, whiskey," Mr Yardley shouted from his drinks cabinet, then made his way over, offering Stewart a glass of the finest whiskey and a firm handshake. "Did I tell you we've had another sixteen managers chasing this position? Well done, young man, well done."

Stewart was delighted to hear that he had beaten sixteen other area managers from around the country but was taken by surprise when Mr Yardley informed him he would need to be in position within two months and asked Stewart if that would cause him any inconvenience. "Not at all," replied Stewart.

"Good, in position by early October and settled in for Christmas, that's what I'd like. The company will deal with all your legal expenses, selling your home and the cost of moving, etc." A few minutes later, Stewart found himself standing outside the main office looking at a very stern-faced secretary.

"I don't believe it, I've just got the best job of my life," he told her.

"Just close the door when you leave, I'm quite busy at the moment," she replied without raising her head. I wonder what makes you happy, Stewart thought as he left the office.

Driving home to celebrate, Stewart knew Jane wasn't going to be too pleased when she found out how little time they had left to get organized, but he needn't have worried, Jane was quite the opposite.

"Never mind," she said. "It is a fantastic opportunity so let's get on with it."

The excitement grew in the Redgrave home, as a moving date got closer. While the children were at school Grandad Freddie and Nanny Debbie arrived to look after them, whilst Stewart and Jane took the opportunity to drive to Cornwall and have a quick look over their new home.

'Hove-To' took Jane's breath away. "Is this really our new home?" she said, stepping out of the car. Its thatched roof, powdery blue window frames and white walls, stood tall on the edge of the coastal path like a beacon to all at sea. Looking from the main bedroom situated at the front of the house, only two other properties could be seen in the distance, a small pink cottage and a little nearer a large white house, at the back of the house was the children's bedrooms, each with its own balcony offering spectacular views along the coast and out to sea, downstairs in the back room, large patio doors would slide open allowing the sea breeze to travel gently through on warm summer days. There was much to take in and organize before returning home.

While their parents were away the children talked about which animals they would like to have. The list read something like this:

three rabbits three ponies to ride, two cows to milk, four goats to keep the grass down, two baby lambs, six piglets and lots and lots of chickens. In big letters it read:

We can only eat the eggs and not the chickens, or any of our pets, Daddy.

Oh and by the way, ducks and geese, Beau wants an elephant but please say no, and one guinea pig please.

The children presented the list to their parents on their return. "I'll keep it in my pocket for safekeeping, you never know," said Stewart as he winked at Grandad.

By the end of the month all the arrangements had been made with schools, the doctor, hospitals and a removal company that would pack and unpack. All they had to do was direct the workmen as to where to place the furniture.

The children agreed that all toys and old clothing no longer required would be donated to their old school's jumble sale to help raise money for computers as a farewell gesture. Nanny and Grandad had been helping for the last few weeks. After a late tea they said their goodbyes and wished them well on the their new adventure.

Jane thanked the children for their support and said how pleased she was that everyone had worked so well together. To be ready two days before the removal vans arrived clearly showed how keen they were. Izabella had tears in her eyes and asked if she would ever see Nanny and Grandad again, Stewart gave her a reassuring cuddle. "Come on, sweetheart, it's only a few hours away by car. Nanny and Grandad will be coming to visit very soon." That helped settle Izabella and it wasn't long before she joined the others looking through old photographs and talking of fond memories late into the night.

Come on, Jane," Stewart called as he ran back into the house. "Hey there you are sweetheart." Jane stood looking at her beautiful garden that had been her source of solitude for many years.

"I'm okay, just saying goodbye to an old friend. We've had wonderful times in this house, it's just been such a safe environment for the children, I've always looked forward to coming home, it's hard to say goodbye, Stewart."

"Hey babe, new times, new adventures, a better life for the children, for all of us."

"I know," said Jane. The removal vans started up.

"It's time to go, sweetheart." Jane closed the front door, kissing her fingertips before placing them gently on the doorframe as a final gesture of love.

"How long will it take us to get there, Daddy?" Izabella asked.

"About four maybe five hours,"

"Let's sing some songs like we do when we travel with Nanny and Grandad, it will make time fly," suggested Izabella. They began to sing the family's favourite songs as they made their way.

Chapter 8
A Lost Friend

Tom had agreed to meet his father at Franklins bar by 8:30 p.m. Ordering a beer he looked at his watch. Tom was pleased to see that he was ten minutes early, time to compose himself, he thought before coming face-to-face with the man who'd pushed him aside for many years. At 9:45 p.m., Tom asked himself why he'd thought it would be any different. Then his mobile rang, better just ignore it than listen to another lame excuse, he thought as he made his way to the exit door. Then he recognized his father coming through another door on the other side of the room. Tom made his way across.

"Ah what time do you call this, son?" Tom's father called out trying to make it sound as if he'd been the one that had been kept waiting.

"I've been here since 8:30 as agreed, you're the one who's late, and I've just seen you come in." His father sensed Tom's annoyance.

"Oh by the way this is Billy, Billy this is my son, Tom." Billy offered to shake Tom's hand but Tom refused it.

"Why do we need him?" Tom asked.

Robin explained. "When I said you'd have no more money worries I meant it, but Billy's a major part of making that happen."

"OK, so start making sense, why should this guy, who I've never met before, have any interest in making me money?" asked Tom.

"Robin," Billy interrupted. "It might be best if I explain."

"Well go-ahead then," said Robin and sat back while Billy told his story.

"Some time ago a friend and I went fishing for a couple of hours off rocks, hoping to catch some sea bass on the evening tide. I dropped him off by boat and he climbed up to his favourite spot. Six hours flew by before I realized the time. When I went back I couldn't see him! His fishing rod was jammed between some rocks. I called out but there was no response, the riptide began to pick up speed, I tried to get in close enough for him to jump back into the boat, but as I said, all I could see was his fishing rod. I stayed calling his name until it was dark. By that time the riptide had got stronger and by 9 o'clock I decided to head for the harbour because the boat had become unstable.

"I had one hand on the tiller and a vice like grip with my other on the side. I'd just about kept me balance; thought I was a gonner to tell the truth. Only with the grace of God and a bit of moonlight did I make my way back to safe waters. Once ashore I made my way quickly along the coastal path, some four miles I reckon, tired I was by the time I got to where he'd been fishing. His rod cast a silhouette against the moonlight, like a beacon it was. I called out again and again but no reply, only then I thought the worst, he'd been taken."

"What do you mean?" asked Tom.

"Taken by the rising water is what I mean."

"Did you call the coastguard?" asked Tom.

"No."

"Why not?"

"I had my reasons," Billy replied.

Tom looked at his father in disbelief.

Billy continued. "Some twelve hours later his wife informed the police that he was missing. Because she didn't know who he'd been fishing with I kept quiet until the police and media lost interest, which they did after his body was washed up a few months later."

"Where?" Tom interrupted.

"Rodney Beach."

"Where's that?" Tom asked. By the expression on his dad's face, Tom knew his dad hadn't a clue, but Billy knew!

"It doesn't matter," said Billy.

"You haven't spoken your mate's name once, why not?" asked Tom.

"It's no concern of yours," came a sharp reply.

"Look, young Tom, I was afraid and still am, I might be done for manslaughter."

"No you wouldn't, taking an adult on a fishing trip doesn't make you responsible for that person, providing you have all the right safety equipment on board and the boat was seaworthy, which it was because you got back! Did you have lifejackets?"

"Well that may be the case, but I wasn't prepared to take that chance," came a cowardly reply.

"Your failure was in not informing the RNLI that someone was lost or in the water, that's everybody's duty." Both men lowered their heads in shame as Tom's clenched fist thumped the table.

The question of lifejackets wasn't answered.

Billy continued, "I go's back a few months later taking a sledge-hammer, metal stake and some rope hoping to find some answers. Lowering myself down I could see his rod still jammed in the rocks his krill and lunchbox were unopened, to the left there was a piece of tightly bound red cloth, it felt strange down there so I didn't stay too long before I made my way back up. At the top I made sure the stake and ropes was hidden good and proper."

"Did you get his fishing rod?" asked Tom.

"No," replied Billy. "I laid his rod down as a mark of respect. Billy then looked around the room before reaching into his pocket, once he was satisfied that no one else had shown any interest in his story he retrieved the red cloth that was lying by the fishing rod.

Billy loosened its knot then pushed it over to Tom. "Take a look, but be careful, lad, it won't do for others to see."

Tom carefully opened the cloth with his fingertips, his eyes widened as he looked upon a gold coin. On one side was a warrior carrying large spear. Robin sat back watching his son's reaction. "What's on the other side?" Tom whispered, as he was about to turn it over.

"No, don't you be touching," said Billy, as he pulled the cloth back and slipped it back into his pocket with great dexterity.

"Where do you think it came from?" enquired Tom.

"I don't think, I know," came the reply. "I went down the cliffs hoping to find clues as to what happened to my mate, had he slipped and injured himself on the rocks below and drowned? I don't know. Just below the waterline some of these were jammed between rocks, a few metres away I could just make out a small cave under the water. Now I've fished there for many years and can honestly say I've never noticed this cave before. Look, there is no guarantee how many are down there but we could be lucky and make a small fortune. I was feeling a bit uneasy on my own so started making my way up but something made me look down, that's when I saw a light."

"What light?" Tom asked.

"Coming from the cave it 'twas only a few seconds mind, then it be gone. I know what I saw I tell ye, there's something down there. I reckon my mate saw something and climbed down that's when he fell."

"If that's the case," Tom interrupted, "explain how the red cloth with the coin was by his fishing gear."

"I reckon he climbed down, got this coin and went back for more. 'Twas on the rocks, I tell you, apart from that I ain't too sure."

Keeping his voice down Billy continued. "In a few months' time 'tis the lowest tide in 100 years, so they say. With the tide so far out it gives us more time to have a good look in the cave, ain't saying no more except, young Tom, are you in or out?"

Tom put his elbows on the table, cupped his chin with both hands and then sat back running his fingers through his fine blond hair until they came to rest at the back of his head, allowing him time to think.

After a long pause Tom said, "OK, count me in."

"Good lad, you won't regret this is," said Robin.

"Right," said Billy. "We'll need someone who can handle a boat just in case Robin can't, someone we can trust, your father said one of your friends might be willing to get involved."

"Just hang on a minute, before I go getting any friends of mine involved I need to make sure this is kosher! Don't we need to register what we find?" asked Tom. Billy informed him that he'd done his research and had somebody standing by ready to shift as many as they find and at a good price.

"Yes I bet you have," replied Tom. "But you didn't answer my question, is this above the law – yes or no?"

"Yes it is," Billy assured him.

"OK, in that case I might be able to help." That brought a smile to Robin's face. "I'll talk to a friend of mine, his family's had boats for years, he will have the experience you're looking for and I know I can trust him. He's going up north soon, I'll put it to him before he goes."

"Right then," Billy began to show some authority, "Tom, I'll leave that to you, have a chat with your mate and let us know if he's interested, but don't give too much away. Robin, you find a boat that's fit for the job, a good engine or two, have them serviced, it will need extra fuel tanks, ropes, lifejackets, flares, radios that sort of thing and give the boat a lick of paint if needed, we don't want it looking shabby and draw attention to ourselves. You'll have sole responsibility so make sure it's right, our lives may depend on it." Robin gave a reassuring nod. But Tom wondered if giving his dad all that responsibility was such a good idea. Billy continued, "I'll need you and your friend to help make a strong cage so we can pick up anything we find, judging by the weight of this coin, we could be in for a heavy load. I'll make all the arrangements and get some local knowledge. Tom, you let me know if your mate's on board. I'll need your mobile number in case I need to contact you, any problems with that?" asked Billy.

"No," replied Tom.

"OK then, you'll have more information later, meanwhile keep this quiet."

Chapter 9
On the Move

Heading south, the Redgrave's satnav informed them that the M5 was coming to an end at the next junction and would be joining the A38-A30 headed south. Stewart soon found himself negotiating narrow lanes with very sharp bends as they travelled deeper into the Cornish countryside, giving way to the occasional combine-harvester, tractors, milk floats and postal vans. Jay was the first awake but stayed quiet, listening to his iPod through his earphones. Beau woke to find Izabella lying sprawled out across him. "Get off me,

Bella," he called out, hoping to get some support from Jay as Izabella woke, saying those immortal words: "Are we there yet?" Jay thought he was missing out on something and removed his earphones, asking if they have far to go.

Ten minutes later they arrived at Hove-To, after travelling six and a half hours, stopping three times for the toilet and once for dinner "There it is!" Stewart called out. The children launched forward trying to be the first to see as the car entered the driveway, no one spoke as they approached their new home and for a few seconds no body moved, they sat in silence peering through misted windows until they couldn't restrain themselves any longer.

The car doors burst open. "Someone let the dogs out!" Jane shouted. Jay opened the back door and together they all raced across the gardens to explore their new surroundings.

The overcast weather made the house look a little tired, its white walls and blue shutters had faded, dead flowers hung over their baskets, partly obscuring the front door. On top of a large chimney the weather vane squeaked as it turned to the prevailing wind, two twisted tree trunks with names, birthdays and hearts neatly carved in them supported a porch which lent slightly to one side.

One that caught Stewart's eye was much deeper than the others, and being inquisitive he removed the moss with a little help of some spit on his fingertips and uncovered a slot the size of a fifty pence piece. But his concentration was broken as three excited children ran by to lay claim to their bedrooms. Jay had the biggest being the eldest, Izabella and Beau's rooms were quite large too and all rooms had their own balcony.

Jay called the others to join him on his, they stood looking out to sea. "look how big the sea is," said Izabella. Beau wondered if anyone lived out there, no one spoke for a while as they listened to a distant boom coming from the sea.

Jay broke the silence, "Come on you lot, let's see who is first to that oak tree."

"Do you know, I've been so busy over the last few months, I'd truly

forgotten how big the kitchen was," said Jane. "It's huge, I've always wanted a big oak table so family and guests could sit down together, debating all sorts of things and listen to lots of stories. I'm so happy, Stewart, look at this lovely big open fireplace a Rayburn, they're great for cooking with and supplying the house with heating and hot water."

Stewart embraced Jane kissing her softly on her cheek. "I'm glad you like it, sweetheart, there's plenty to do but it shouldn't take long to get settled and call it home, let's have a look at the front room before the furniture arrives."

"Good idea," said Jane.

"Yes I remember now, saying how much I liked the big bay window and the fireplace. As you said, the room is quite square," said Jane, looking at the height of the ceiling.

"It's going to take some heating in the winter."

"Well the Rayburn, central heating and an open fire should cope, don't you think? We're not going to be cold, Stewart," Jane reassured him.

"Yes, you're right, love. We're going to need more plug sockets for computers, etc., not that I'm thinking there's any chance of an Internet connection down here just yet. We must let the children know but suggest we cross that bridge when we come to it. They're bound to ask sooner or later, what are your thoughts, Jane?"

"Yes I agree with most of what you say except…" Jane was about to continue when she pointed to the window. The removal van was making its way slowly down the dirt track swaying from side to side like a yacht in rough seas; through the front gates it finally stopped outside the front door.

"I'll go and greet them," said Stewart. "Call the children, Jane, I'm sure they'd like to help. Let's get this done as quickly as possible before it gets dark."

"Come on you two," Jay called, arriving first at the oak, behind it stood an old wooden shed with its door hanging off its hinge, some branches from the oak tree had punctured its roof and others had speared them through the windows in some past violent storm. Inside, old lawnmowers, garden tools, books, cardboard boxes, a filing cabinet and a table with all sorts of things shoved on top and underneath. Chairs had been rammed in to every corner, some chairs had broken legs or ripped covers. Outside, rubbish from previous owners was stacked high, the whole area had become a dumping ground for many years.

"Let's explore," shouted Izabella as she ran through the large overgrown garden with the dogs in close pursuit.

By the kitchen door was a patio, to the left a flowerbed and a small waterfall that ran into a fishpond containing four large goldfish. They heard their mother calling from the balcony. "Children, the removal van has arrived, so all hands on deck please."

By 10:30 p.m. the furniture removal van had left and the children had been fed showered and were on their way to bed. Stopping at the foot of the stairs, Jay asked his father if they could use the old shed as their secret place.

"What shed?" Stewart asked.

"It's at the back of the oak tree, but we will need your help to repair it, Daddy, please." On the landing Izabella and Beau stood statue-like listening, waiting for their father's response.

"I can't see a problem with that, I'm off work for a week or two so I'll have a look at it when I get a chance, but for now goodnight, Jay."

Izabella called out, "We'll have a secret password, Daddy, but you and Mummy can't know what it is, it's a secret."

"OK children, off to bed now please."

Beau paused at his bedroom door. "You OK, Beau?" Jay asked, Izabella tiptoed down the landing to join them.

"What's wrong?" asked Izabella.

Beau told them that when he tried to come out of the bedroom earlier the door wouldn't open, it kept pulling against him, it opened a little bit then slammed shut. "I felt cold and called out to you, Izabella, but you didn't hear me. I got very scared and put my hands over my face and started to cry. Then the door opened by itself," he said. "Would it be OK if I sleep with you, just for tonight, Jay, please?" Before Jay had a chance to answer Izabella said she too was scared and wanted to join them.

"OK, but this will be our first secret. In the morning you must go back to your own bedrooms before Mummy and Daddy find out."

Jay gave Beau's door a gentle nudge, it remained closed until they reached his bedroom. Looking back, Jay saw Beau's bedroom door open by itself. He decided not to say anything to the others. In bed, Jay whispered, "Tomorrow we will prick our fingers and become blood brothers and sister then we can think of the secret password."

"Not me," whispered Izabella, making it clear that she had no intention of pricking her finger.

"Well, that's up to you, Bella," said Jay quietly.

"Does your finger bleed when you prick it?" asked Beau.

"Yes, just a little bit, then it stops."

"Look," said Jay, "if you don't, then you can't be a member of our secret society."

"OK, I'll do it," said Beau, Izabella didn't reply. The children fell asleep.

Chapter 10
Billy's Operation

In the café a week later Tom explained to Paul what the meeting with his father had been about and asked if he wanted to be part of the plan. Without any hesitation Paul jumped at the idea. "Sounds exciting to me, I'll give it a go, count me in. I can handle all sorts of boats so no worries there, mate," said Paul.

Tom's phone rang. "It's Billy! Yes, I'm with him now he wants in. No! Look, the only way this will work is for me to come and make a start, yes on my own; Paul can join me after Christmas."

"Any problems?" Paul asked. Tom raised his hand to stop him from interrupting as he listened carefully to what Billy had to say.

"No worries, OK, I agree with that – OK – we'll team up after Christmas then," Billy ended the call.

"Build a cage?" Paul enquired.

"In case we come across anything heavy, apparently we need two people to build it, Billy's going in for an operation and won't be fit until after Christmas."

"Did he say what his problem was?" Paul asked.

"No. And it's not my place to ask," Tom replied.

"What about your dad?" Paul asked.

"My old man's useless at this sort of thing so we've agreed to leave it until you're back home or Billy's fit enough. He'll make contact when he's ready."

Graham arrived with the boys' breakfast and told them the big guy had been seen quite a few times looking in the window, unfortunately by the time he'd got to the front door he'd gone.

"It doesn't bother me, Graham. He won't stop us coming in," said Tom.

"That's my boys," Graham replied, not wishing to lose any of his loyal customers, then went about clearing tables.

Chapter 11
It's Christmas

The school bus began its daily routine of collecting children from farms, hamlets and isolated homes. The Redgrave's were always last to be picked up at 7:45 a.m., and the last to be dropped off at 17:45 p.m. Though the journey seemed to take forever, good friendships were formed which helped the children settle into their new school.

Before Stewart began his new job at the forestry he kept the promise he'd made to the children and repaired the garden shed. "There's one condition before I hand over the keys," Stewart told them. "If Mummy and Daddy feel the need to enter your secret den for safety reasons we must be allowed to do so." The children thought it over then agreed it was for the best.

By the 23rd of December the new house had been decorated from top to toe. Nanny and Grandad had arrived to spend the holiday with the family and on Christmas morning the house was filled with excitement as the children ran into their parents' bedroom. Unaware of the time they gently tapped them to ask if it was time to go downstairs. Mummy and Daddy lay very still pretending to be fast asleep, then at the same time they sat up shouting, "Merry Christmas!!" After hugs and kisses, Daddy whispered, "Go and wake Nanny and Grandad." So off they went charging along the landing and burst into their grandparents' bedroom.

"It's Christmas!" they shouted. "You've got to wake up! Come on Nanny and Grandad, it's Christmas!" Nanny was already awake and jumped out of bed like one of the children.

"Come on, Grandad," she called, "It's presents time."

Grandad rolled over and looked at his watch. "It's only six o'clock," he yawned. "It's too early, far too early."

"Come on, Grandad it's time," said Jay. Taking him by the hand, Izabella and Beau led a very sleepy Grandad gently down the stairs.

The morning was spent opening lots of presents and by late afternoon the smell of Christmas dinner had engulfed the whole house. Jane called out, "Dinner's ready everyone."

Sitting around the big oak table they began pulling crackers and telling the awful jokes, after eating far too much, Stewart and Grandad retired to the living room and fell asleep in front of the fire while Jane and Nanny read magazines and ate chocolates, and the children played quietly with their new toys. After evening tea, everyone was truly stuffed and the family's games were put on hold until seven o'clock and didn't finish until late that evening.

The following day was Boxing Day and for many years the family had their traditional walk in Sutton Park, Birmingham. Keen to keep the tradition alive the coast path was chosen for their first Christmas walk in their new surroundings. They soon became exposed to the full force of the prevailing south-westerly blowing in from the Atlantic Ocean. The winds blew onshore generating huge waves that crashed onto the rocks below creating a fine mist that raced up the cliff-face, then rolled over the top and chilled the air as it left a fine dampness on everything it touched.

After two hours feeling cold and damp a decision was made to head for home. Holding on to their hats they turned into a cold headwind and began their struggle home. Grandad said he was feeling cold and ready for a drink or two! (No, Not Cider) Just a nice cup of tea is all he fancied, until later!

By the time they'd reached home it was dark, inside they were met with that wonderful smell of burning wood and the sound of crackling and sputtering coming from a guarded fire that Stewart had prepared earlier. For a moment they stood in silence without any light on, watching the long orange flames casting their rhythmic dance across the walls and ceilings, the Christmas tree too played its part as the baubles reflected hundreds of mini coloured fires. It wasn't long before they all felt warmed and ready for tea, followed by a few games before bedtime. At ten o'clock the children made their way up to bed. "Can we have one of Grandad's magical stories as a special Christmas treat, please?" Jay asked. The three children cuddled up in Jay's bed. After a long day packed with lots of excitement and that exhilarating walk home, it wasn't long before they'd drifted off into their own wonderlands.

After having such a busy time settling in, Jane and Stewart were looking forward to the New Year. They'd marked this as their new beginning and a fresh start for all the family. The children felt Christmas had gone by far too quickly. Nanny and Grandad had gone back home and the decorations had been put away for another year. The house felt empty as they looked through frosty windows wishing for an early spring, but the cold spell tightened its grip turning weeks slowly into long boring months.

Chapter 12
A Smuggler's Song

It was late February by the time Billy rang Tom to arrange a meeting in the Ship Inn. Tom hadn't heard from Paul so decided to give him a call. "Hi mate, I've just received a call from Billy, he wants to arrange a meeting at the Ship Inn at 8 on Friday evening, are you still up for this, mate?" Tom asked.

"Yes, I'm on my way home tomorrow, arriving at Penzance at 11 p.m. perhaps we could grab a coffee Thursday morning."

"Can't do, got a couple of job interviews on Thursday so we'll meet up with the rest on Friday night, sorry mate."

"That's OK," said Paul. "That's cool with me, I know the pub so I'll see you there, best of luck job hunting, mate."

It was gone 8:30 p.m. when Robin joined the others, apologizing for being late. Some things never change, Tom thought! The lads moved in closer to hear what Billy had to say.

"OK lads, I'll have to keep my voice down so listen carefully. I've got some information on tides, it's definitely going to be the lowest in years and that's what we've been waiting for. We'll be able to get deeper into the cave, but once that tide turns she comes in fast and strong, so we'll need to keep an eye on the water levels at all times. I've made contact with some locals but it's not been easy, they aren't keen on outsiders and tend to keep themselves to themselves. Look," said Billy as he opened a small map. "This old map shows a sunken ship. Now, locals believe she was carrying gold coins on her way up to London and some say she was shipwrecked." Billy took it upon himself to give a quick history lesson.

"Two hundred years ago this village like all other small villages along the coast, it depended on smuggling spirits, tobacco, silks and wine. Anything they brought ashore this way would avoid customs and excise duty. Mevagissey was renowned for smuggling and ship-wrecking; on dark stormy nights they'd swing their oil-filled lanterns indicating a safe passage to ships. Unaware of their betrayal the ships followed blindly until they ran aground and were torn apart by rough seas and jagged rocks. Most of the crew drowned, those that survived were quickly dealt with on the beach while the smugglers helped themselves to the bounty. They say the whole village was involved, that's some two hundred folk – including police, clergymen and judges, but nobody talks about it these days."

After a pause, he went on: "The poem by Rudyard Kipling, 'A Smuggler's Song' says it all really and shows how important it was to keep your secrets and to mind your own business or pay the price.

If you awake at midnight and hear the horses feet,
Don't go drawing back the blinds, or looking in the street.
Them that ask no questions isn't told a lie.
Watch the wall, my darling, while the Gentleman go by!
Five and twenty ponies,
Trotting through the dark-
Brandy for the parson,
Baccy for the Clark;
Laces for a lady, letters for a spy,
And watch the wall, my darling, while the gentlemen go by!
Running round the woodlump if you chance to find
Little barrels, roped and tarred, all full of brandy-wine,
Don't you shout to come and look, nor use 'em for your play.
Put the brushwood back again-and they'll be gone next day

"I tell you this so that when we talk we talk in whispers. No one must know what we're up to, do you understand!" Billy asked, as he looked around the table.

The lads began to realize that Billy knew a thing or two and had everything under control.

He continued, "I think over the years that the coins got washed further along the coast. Some ended up in the cave. If these coins are the same my mate picked up we could be in for a small fortune."

"How many are there," asked Tom.

"That's anyone's guess."

"Robin," said Billy, "you bring us up to date now with what you've been up to."

"Err so far I've spent £878.63."

"On what exactly?" Billy asked.

"Well, we now have a rib, I've chosen it because they're safe and stable on water and two fifty horse powered engines, which I'm working on at the moment, it'll give us plenty of power when we need it. I'm keeping my eyes open for some rope, second-hand life-jackets, diesel-containers, oars, storage bins, flares, radios and tools.

I'm trying to keep the cost down but it's not easy."

Tom interrupted, "Have you got receipts?"

"No I haven't," said Robin with slight annoyance in his voice. "I don't keep receipts, son."

"Well you do from now on," said Billy.

"Look, you don't have to pay now, we'll settle the bill when we split the gold." Tom gave his father a hard stare.

"OK," said Billy, "about the cage, I don't expect you two to start building it just yet, it's far too cold for that. I'll give you my address then in April or May it doesn't matter which, you both come and make a start. I'll have the supplies so we should be ready by late July. If everyone agrees let's make a date for our next meeting." They checked their diaries and agreed on the 17th of June.

Chapter 13
Sister? And Blood Brothers

When Stewart arrived home he found the front door wide open. "Hi," he shouted as he threw his jacket towards the coat stand, missing as usual. I'll get that one day, he thought as he placed the car keys on the key safe, "Where is everybody?"

"I'm in the kitchen," replied Jane. "Just sorting out tea."

"Hi baby, have you had a good day?"

"Yes it's been fine, the children have been outside since breakfast, only came in for a quick sandwich around lunchtime, I've not seen them since. I've managed to get on with what I wanted to do and even found time to make a start on the allotment."

"That's good news, I know you've been longing to make a start."

"Yeah, I'm a bit late this year but the summer's finally arrived and in a few months it will be time to start sewing winter crops so there's plenty to do."

"Jane, did you know the front door was wide open?"

"No I didn't! I thought I shut it after saying goodbye to our visitor."

"Who was that?"

"A guy named Phil Hilldridge, he runs the local garage and called to say a quick hello, if we need any repairs to our car or driveway we're to give him a call."

"Well that's very neighbourly of him."

"He's from that big white house at the top of the lane. I thanked him and asked if he would like to come in for a coffee but he said he was too busy at the moment, he's invited us to their barbecue in June."

"That sounds great, Jane, a chance to get to know our neighbours."

"His wife's called Ann, they have two girls Nicola and Carrie and they're younger than ours I think! I thanked him for the invitation and he just said 'no worries, that's how we work round here, looking after each other'. He's a big chap with a big black beard. When we shook hands I noticed how big they were, I wouldn't want to fall out with you, I thought."

"Me neither by the sounds of it. I'll go and see what the children are up to," said Stewart.

"Before you do, let me tell you something funny that happened today. While I was in the garden, Jay and Beau had gone inside their secret den, Izabella was locked outside, apparently she'd forgotten the password. She became really angry with herself and started banging and kicking the door shouting this password is really silly. At one point I thought she was going to break the door down. Thankfully she remembered the magic word Shondablur! God only knows what that means, but that's what she shouted and the door opened, but before she entered, the cheeky little madam stopped and studied me! As if I was the enemy, obviously making sure she hadn't given the game away. I pretended I hadn't heard anything of course, but thank goodness she finally got it right."

"She's a proper madam all right," said Stewart with a smile on his face.

The children were busy cleaning out their den. After moving lots of rubbish the rusting cabinet was next. Using old branches from the oak tree to act as levers the children pushed and pulled at different angles as they attempted to move it across the floor. After twenty minutes the boys agreed that it was too heavy to move.

"Why don't we empty the drawers, taking them out will make it lighter!" suggested Izabella. The boys thought she was quite mad and decided to carry on struggling for another ten minutes, finally they accepted they weren't going to win and reluctantly emptied the drawers, but still the cabinet was too heavy.

"Flipping heck," said Beau. "What's this made of?"

"I don't know," said Jay, huffing and puffing as he used a metal bar he'd found behind some cardboard boxes. Then the cabinet began to give way inch by inch. Once they were happy with its new location they sat on boxes to catch their breath while Izabella swept the floor.

The air filled with a fine dust so they decided to wait outside until the air cleared. Back inside they began putting things back on the shelves. Beau's elbow caught an old vase and knocked it off the table. "Don't worry, I'll sweep it up," said Beau, and he began to sweep up the mess.

Jay shouted, "Stop, look!" Carefully kneeling down Jay pointed to the outline of a trap door, at the same time he told Izabella to close the shed door – just as their father arrived outside.

"Hi you guys, how's it going in there?" They looked at the door then at each other.

Jay answered, "Hi Dad, we're fine, just having some fun."

"Okay, don't be too long, tea's nearly ready."

They waited until the coast was clear. "Drag that table over here," Jay told them, "and put some boxes underneath that will hide the trap door until we return tomorrow – and not a word to anyone. Tomorrow we become blood brothers and sister. Remember, Izabella, if you don't share blood you can't be a blood sister." Izabella gave Jay that look and then slammed the door behind her.

In the den the following morning, Jay pulled a needle from his pocket, one he'd taken from his mother's sewing kit. "One of us has to be the leader," said Jay. "I'm the oldest so I suggest that's me." They agreed.

Izabella was first to roll up her sleeves and turned slightly to one side biting on her bottom lip as she offered up her arm, Jay smiled. "You're not having a needle, Bella, it's just a finger prick."

Beau loosened his trainers. "Why are you doing that?" Izabella asked.

"It's so I can cross my toes when I feel the prick on my finger, I don't like needles."

"Oh," said Izabella looking slightly puzzled.

"OK Beau, you're next." Beau moved forward, did a bit of fidgeting while he crossed his toes, and closed his eyes. "That's it! Beau, it's all over," said Jay. He gave a big smile and slowly opened one eye after the other. Jay did his without any fuss at all then squeezed their fingers to draw more blood to mix on a piece of paper.

"Before we put this in the envelope," said Jay, "we must repeat this together, we do this now to keep our secrets safe." Holding hands they chanted. We do this now to keep our secrets safe. Then Jay put the paper into an envelope and sealed it, folding it tightly before hiding it under the floorboards somewhere!

The following morning their father had gone off to work and Mummy was busy in the house, the coast was clear to return to their den. Inside, Jay noticed a piece of rope attached to the trap door. "We'll all need to pull hard to break the seal. Come on! Pull harder," Jay called out. It took a few attempts but eventually the door opened.

"It looks very dark down there," Beau whispered. "I think we're going to need some torches. Bella, you know where they are but don't let Mummy see you, hurry!" Jay ordered.

Five minutes later Izabella stood panting as if she'd just won the Olympics. "How many did you get?"

"Two," Izabella replied.

"That's going to have to do then."

"Well there isn't any more, Jay. Have a look yourself if you don't believe me."

"Let's follow the steps and see where they take us," Beau said as he gathered ropes, an old knife and a hammer.

"Why do we need them?" Bella enquired.

"It's always best to go prepared," said Jay.

"Prepared! For what, Jay," asked Bella.

"Anything," replied Beau. "First we need to lock the shed door."

"Good idea," said Jay. "Let's put this iron bar across."

"No! Don't do that," said Izabella. "Mummy and Daddy have given their word they won't enter the den unless they feel we're in danger, so there's no need to put a bar across the door is there?" The boys agreed.

"OK this is how it's going to work," said Jay. "We leave the table in the corner over the trapdoor. We'll be able to lift the door high enough for us to squeeze through when we go down and when we come out it will close behind us. If we keep these cardboard boxes on the floor nobody's going to see the trap door anyway."

"That makes more sense," said Bella.

Jay was the first to go down into the darkness; they'd only gone a short distance when a deafening boom made them jump. "That's the sound we heard from the balcony," whispered Bella as a strong wind rushed past them. Frozen to the spot they listened hard, trying to figure out where the sound was coming from.

Jay turned and looked back, as he did his torch lit the faces of Bella and Beau. "Do you want to carry on?" he whispered.

"I don't know," said Bella.

"What about you, Beau?"

"I don't like being at the back, I can't see where I'm going because I haven't got a torch."

"Bella, would you swap places? Then the light from your torch will shine in front of you and give enough light for Beau to see where he's going."

"I don't mind, I'm not frightened!" said Izabella. "But does that mean we're going to carry on?" At that precise moment another boom came rushing up from the darkness, this time it wasn't so loud and only a gentle breeze followed, but Izabella wasn't having any of it and dropped her torch as she ran back up to the trapdoor followed closely by Beau.

Jay called out to them, "That's twice we've heard that boom and it hasn't done us any harm, has it? It's safe, just follow me," Jay reassured them. They continued down underneath their garden, heading for the cliffs. Deeper and deeper they went until they reached a door. On the right, someone had made a box out of driftwood, inside they found neatly coiled ropes, tools, boat hooks and four candles.

"It must have been a tool store for someone, we'll make it ours from now on," said Jay.

"This door hasn't been opened for a long time," said Beau.

"Just a minute," said Izabella, "we don't know what's behind the door, we could be in danger."

The boys shrugged their shoulders and began pulling at the door while Izabella held the torch, after a lot of moaning and groaning the door finally gave way, opening in to a massive cave.

"Woah!" Izabella called out, her echo seemed never ending. "This is massive! Look how high we are."

"Yes we'll have to be careful if we're going to climb down," said Jay as another boom filled the air followed by a light gust of wind. "Don't worry, I think I know what it is," said Jay.

"What then?" asked Izabella.

"It's waves hitting the entrance to this cave that's making the noise, which in turn generates the wind that brings the smell of the sea air through the cave."

"I thought it was a monster," said Beau, swallowing hard.

"Me too, I was ready to go back," said Izabella.

"You did go back!" said Jay. Beau dipped his head, keeping quiet; Izabella pushed her tongue against the inside of her cheek and shrugged her shoulders.

After tying a rope to a big rock they lowered themselves down to the cave floor and headed for the distant daylight. Water constantly dripped from the ceiling and ran down the walls making it difficult to walk. They soon began to feel cold and damp as they continued on until they reached the mouth of the cave. Standing on a sandy beach in bright sunshine they looked up at the cliffs and were amazed how far down the tunnel had taken them. Waves crashed against the rocks sending a fine spray of cold water into the air soaking them even more.

"Best make our way back," said Jay.

On the way back they hadn't realized they'd passed the rope, which they'd used to climb down, and went deeper into the cave. The light from Izabella's torch caught the edge of a big hole on the cave's floor. Standing right on the edge of a deep ledge, one more step, just one, and that would have been the end for Izabella. Luckily her gymnastics saved her, only Izabella had the skills to spin round without losing her balance and step away so calmly.

A big hole ran almost the width of the cave's floor. "Stay where you are," she told them as she carefully took one step back at a time. Looking down she noticed something shining in the mud and knelt down to pick it up; giving it a quick glance she put it in her pocket. Jay shone his touch down the abyss to see how deep it was but the beam from his torch wasn't strong enough and faded before it reached the bottom. The fact that no one had fallen in was a miracle.

"OK everyone take your time, keep stepping back slowly until you're sure you're clear," said Jay.

They made their way back, trying to find the rope. "There it is!" Beau called out.

Arriving back in their den with wet clothes and muddy boots they felt tired and cold. "This is our first big secret, we tell no one," said Jay.

"If Daddy found out we would be in for it," said Izabella.

"I'm not sure," said Beau.

"What do you mean you're not sure?" said Bella.

"I didn't think I'd ever have to keep secrets this big before, I don't know if I can!"

"Yes you can," said Jay. "There's no danger, we can keep going down and have lots of fun exploring, we're not doing anything naughty."

"I gave my blood today, Beau, " Izabella said raising her voice. "I didn't do that for nothing! We have to keep this secret."

Beau realized Izabella wasn't happy and simply said, "OK."

"Where on earth have you been?" mother asked. "I've been calling you for ages, you've missed your dinner and it's time for tea. Your father will be home any minute now so you'd better go and get yourselves cleaned up, look at the mud on your shoes! Take them off before you go inside please."

At the table, Stewart asked the children what they'd been up to. "Oh just playing football," said Jay.

"We've made a tree den," said Izabella.

"My word you have been busy, what about Beau?"

"You'll never guess what we found in our secret den, Daddy!"

Before he could utter another word he received a sharp kick from under the table. Jay and Izabella's eyes widened as they stared at Beau, wondering if he was about to expose their secret. Beau gave Jay a sharp kick back, "Ouch! It wasn't me it was Izabella," Jay shouted.

Stewart intervened. "Now, Beau you're not going to tell me what you found! That would spoil your secret wouldn't it?"

"Yes Daddy, I know that. I wasn't going to tell you what we really found I was going to make something up."

"Oh, I see," said Stewart, winking at Jane before asking her if she'd been listening to the radio today.

"Only this morning, why?"

"We have an American survey ship in the docks called Wild-Thing with lots of sophisticated equipment on board, apparently she's looking for an old ship that went down many years ago. They don't know if she was shipwrecked or hit rocks and sank. Apparently she had 16 cannons on board so quite a big ship, they know from records she was carrying wine, silk, tobacco and large amounts of gold and silver coins."

"How much gold?" Jay asked.

"They haven't said, but they'll find her."

"Why is it called Wild-Thing, Daddy?" Beau asked.

"When I was a young boy there was a song called Wild Thing by the Troggs, maybe the owner liked the music so much he named the ship after it."

"Did you like the song, Daddy?" asked Izabella.

"Yes I did, it was one of my favourites. In those days I used to dress like a hippie and dance really crazy."

"Like when you dance now, Daddy, and embarrass us?" asked Jay.

"No even worse," said Jane. The children laughed.

"Why, don't they leave the gold and let English people find it?" Izabella asked.

"Well they used to in the old days, then it was called smuggling. People from around here used the caves to hide everything they'd taken from the big ships and store it, it was called bounty. When the coast was clear they used pulleys and ropes to bring all the treasures up to the top of the cliff. Some say they had hidden caves even secret tunnels but no one has ever found one, they now think that part of history was made up.

The children stopped eating, their knives and forks clenched tight in their hands as they listened to their father's every word. "Today, as long as you've had permission from which ever country you're in – whether under the sea or on dry land anywhere in the world. In fact you can look, but if you find anything you become liable to pay the duty (a tax) to whichever country it's found in."

"Even just a bit," asked Izabella.

"It depends what you mean by a bit," said Stewart.

"Just one coin, would you have to pay then?"

"I don't think you would, why? You haven't got one have you?" Stewart said jokingly.

Izabella burst into tears. "Oh come now, Daddy's only joking, don't take it so seriously," said Jane as she gave her a big cuddle. "So that's what's been on the horizon for the last few days?" asked Jane.

"Yes, don't you think it's exciting?"

"I'd be more excited if I had some of the treasure," Jane replied.

In her bedroom that night, Izabella began to wash the dirt off the coin she'd found in the cave. Rubbing hard she broke through the grime to find a beautiful gold coin, on one side was a man carrying a large spear on the other side a child's face with a teardrops falling from one eye, and written around the edge it read: Protector of Honesty. Izabella's hands began to shake. Protector of Honesty, what does this mean? she thought. This must have come from the sunken ship Daddy had spoken about.

She jumped into bed and began to wonder if it was safe to keep it. We haven't paid any of that duty, I don't want Mummy and Daddy to get into trouble, she thought. Her head began to spin, filling her mind with all sorts of strange things until she fell into a deep sleep, dreaming of pirates sailing on the open seas.

On board Destiny the first mate had stolen a gold coin from the captain's cabin. "Just for entering my quarters without my permission," said the captain, "I'd tie you to the main mast and give you one hundred lashings, but my friend, you stole from me and for that you walk the plank!" The pleads for mercy went unheard. "Tie this thief's hands and fill its pockets with stones!" the captain shouted. "You'll sink to the bottom of the sea with the rest of the scum never to be seen again." Still pleading for his life, they pushed the thief along the plank using long poles, as the thief sank below the water, Izabella woke from her dream gasping for air, her nightmare was over. In the dead of night she left her bed and emptied one of her jewellery boxes and placed the coin inside.

She opened her bedroom window and threw the box out, as it fell to the ground below, the box and coin separated, the coin hit a piece of rockery causing something from inside it to shoot out across the garden before burying itself in the soft soil, the box bounced and lay between the roses. Before falling back to sleep, Izabella had decided she wouldn't tell anyone about the coin. That way, she thought, she'd be keeping everyone safe.

Chapter 14
Could Billy Be Trusted?

"Just a minute, lads," said Billy. "I'll get my neighbour to help put the cage on the back of the wagon, I can't do any heavy lifting because of my operation, but I have to say you've done a good job there, boys. Put this metal box inside the cage. It's for keeping things safe. "

They drove to the docks where they found Robin hard at work on the rib.

"Morning, Robin!" Billy shouted from the pontoon. "The boys are here with the cage, we need to put it on the rib and secure it, how's everything going here?"

"Not too bad," Robin replied. "All the paintwork's done. I've got the engines and suppliers sorted."

"Well done," said Billy. The boys arrived with the cage.

"Morning lads," said Robin.

"Morning!" they both replied.

Had things started to settle between Tom and his father? Or was Tom just pleased with the work he had done on the cage and was simply in a good mood? "Did you paint those shark teeth on the side of the rib, Dad?" asked Tom.

"No son, that's not my art work, they were already on and unfortunately I can't get them off. I agree they look a bit sinister but I'm afraid we're going to have to live with it."

In glorious sunshine they worked as a team preparing the rib and getting the supplies ready.

"Paul!" Billy called out. "Would you mind picking up some refreshments and a newspaper for me, lad?"

"No problem," said Paul.

On his return they sat on the beach drinking and eating sandwiches while they planned their next move. Robin picked up the newspaper. "Hey Billy, you'd better have a look at this."

Leaning into the boat, Billy took the newspaper from Robin. On the front page was a picture of the research vessel in the bay at Mevagesey.

"What's wrong?" asked Paul.

"Just a minute," said Billy. "I need to read this. Damn! Damn! Damn! They're after the same ship – hoping to find its treasure."

"Who is?" Tom demanded.

"Wild-Thing," said Robin. "It's an American research vessel in the bay,"

"No!" Tom shouted in disbelief.

Billy finished reading the article and slammed the newspaper closed. "Right lads," he said, "we don't know if they've found anything yet, we don't know whether they've even started looking, I think it's best we bring our trip forward."

"Hang on, Billy, correct me if I'm wrong but didn't you say we needed to wait for the lowest tides so we could get deeper into the cave, and it would be much safer for us then? Am I right? Isn't that what you said?" Paul asked.

Robin sensed Billy was struggling to find an answer and came to his rescue. "Lads, if you'd known Bill as long as me, you'll know he always airs on the side of caution."

"What does that mean exactly?" Tom asked.

"He believes in safety first. Look," said Robin, "we'll all have to agree on any decisions we make so if anyone is not happy you know what to do. This rib will float on less than a metre of water, we can pull it inside the cave while we look for the treasure. As we walk along using these leggings, they'll keep us dry and if the water gets too deep we simply jump into the rib and use the engines to get us out, it's as simple as that. If we don't move fast these Americans will take the lot. Is that what you want? asked Robin.

Chapter 15
At the White House

The family had spent the day at Phil Hilldrige's barbecue and having had a long, exhausting day the children were tucked up in bed. "Have you seen the dogs, Stewart?" Jane asked.

"Yes they're on the landing outside the children's bedrooms, they're OK there for tonight."

"I think Baxter and Toby have finally settled down in their new surroundings, don't you?"

"Yes I do," said Stewart. "That was a lovely day and what a nice family, I must try and remember their names, you know what I'm like for forgetting… Phil, Ann, Nicola and er Carrie."

"Well done," said Jane. "I have to say the White House is impressive from the outside but inside it's absolutely fabulous and that swimming pool is to die for."

"Yes, I was quite impressed myself. Changing the subject, love, don't forget I'm away until Thursday sorting out a few problems at head office."

Before Jane answered, the phone rang. Taking the call Jane looked puzzled as she passed the phone over to Stewart, "It's work," she whispered.

"What, at this hour?" said Stewart quietly.

He listened carefully, shaking his head saying only a few words then replaced the receiver.

"What's wrong?" asked Jane.

"It's Mr Yardley, he's been involved in a bad car accident."

"Is he alright?"

"I don't know the full details but it sounds bad, they're asking all managers to cover his work for a month at a time until he's fit enough to return. I've been selected to cover the first month."

"Who's going to cover your work while you're away?"

"Apparently that's been taken care of, young Peter will take over until I'm back, he's quite capable so there won't be a mess to sort out when I get back."

"I can see you're not keen on the idea but at least you'll get yours out the way first, then you'll be back by the end of July early August and have the rest of the summer here. I'll be all right with the children so don't worry. They've got plenty to occupy their minds here, just keep in contact from time to time."

"I'll be gone before the children wake, tell them I love them and I'm going to miss you all, let them know I'll phone when I can. I never expected anything like this, sweetheart."

"Don't worry, it can't be helped. Just keep in contact when you can."

Stewart left early the following morning, unaware just how serious Mr Yardley's injuries were.

Chapter 16
Trouble On-board

The lads meet in the Harbor View café, as planned.

"Don't you think the wind's a bit strong?" Paul asked.

"It will ease off within the next hour or so, until it does we'll stay here," Billy reassured him. "In the meantime let's put the final bit on the rib."

Tom rejoined the others, after overhearing a conversation in the newsagents. "Lads, you'll never guess what I've just heard. Wild-Thing put two divers on the seabed yesterday, one brought back a hand full of old coins, they reckon the other ones got carried away by the riptide and they haven't found him yet. That's what the bloke in the newsagents said, then the local postman came in and told everyone he'd heard the coins had a man with a spear on one side and the face of a child on the other. Apparently Wild-Thing isn't going anywhere."

"And why's that?" Billy asked.

"A fire broke out last night wiping out some of her computers so she's stuck there for another month or so before she can resume her search. They say that ever since they located the shipwreck there's been nothing but trouble on-board."

"In that case we could stick to our original plans and go at the end of August," said Paul.

"No," said Billy. "This is just hearsay, we don't know how long it's going to take to repair the computers. If we miss this opportunity, as Robin said, we get nothing. I suggest we carry on, wait till this wind drops and make our move, it's now or never. Are you in, Tom?"

"Yes."

"Robin?"

"Yes."

"Paul?"

"Something's telling me we should wait, so I'm saying no, I'm sorry to let you down."

"That's OK," said Billy. "Best we know now and thanks for your honesty and your help, can we ask you not to say anything to anybody while we go ahead?"

"Of course you can, you have my word."

Just then a Range Rover from the RNLI's, coastal watch pulled up, the driver made his way across to them.

"Tell me you're not thinking of going out to sea in these conditions, lads?" he asked.

Billy was quick to assure him that they were just getting the rib ready for a future trip. "I'm happy to hear that, we've already lost a diver from that research vessel. The high tides have generated strong under-currents and we don't want to lose any more lives, do we?!" Bidding them a good morning he returned to his vehicle. Billy suggested the need to regroup tomorrow and make a start in the morning at 10 o'clock, Tom and Robin agreed.

Chapter 17
The Skeleton

After breakfast Jane told the children that Daddy had to go away on business and wouldn't be back for a month.

"Is it to do with work, Mummy?" asked Izabella.

"Yes, sweetheart, Daddy will be back soon, so don't you worry."

The boys seemed to accept the situation and hadn't much to say on the matter. They had other things on their minds.

Inside the cave they ventured deeper as they made their way along a thin ledge. Beau looked down. "Look over there, there's something shining in the water."

Izabella knew what they were but said nothing. "Whatever they are," said Jay, "we can't reach them, it's too dangerous."

"Jay, can you see those hooks in the rocks?"

"Yes, Izabella, there's some by the door, there's lots of them in the rocks too."

"Quiet. Someone's coming," Beau whispered.

"It's Baxter and Toby," shouted Izabella. With the dogs they felt more confident and ventured deeper, a shaft of light coming from a hole in the cave's roof helped them along their way until they reached a dead end. Pushed high against the back wall, fishing nets of different colours clung to the rocks like cobwebs, trapping plastic containers of different shapes and sizes. Among them lay dead seabirds, driftwood, bits of rope and oil drums. Thousands of broken seashells covered the floor, contributing to a very strong pungent smell that lingered in a fine mist. Every step echoed a thousand times.

Something spooked Baxter and Toby, their barking became so

loud the children had to put their hands over their ears to protect them.

"Quiet!" shouted Izabella as she made her way over to see what all the excitement was about. Then the cave filled with a shattering scream as she came across a skeleton. It was holding a torch tightly in its right hand, a final act of comfort before the light faded.

Jay and Beau ran across to her, Beau was about to reach for the torch. "No, don't touch it, it's time to go," said Jay.

"Who do you think it was?" asked Izabella.

"How do you expect me to know?" said Jay. "But it can't be a pirate, that's for sure."

"Why not?" Beau asked.

"Because pirates didn't have torches, did they!"

On the way back, Beau spotted something and called Jay over. "Look, it's an old telescope. Do you think it's from the old ship?" asked Beau.

"Maybe. Everyone stand still!" Jay listened. "That's water! The tide has turned, we need to get out of here and I mean right now!" Jay said firmly. Back at the big hole they were surprised by the amount of water cascading down the hole in the floor. It looked angry now as it shot over the hole filling the back of the cave.

The sound was overpowering, Jay had to shout at the top of his voice to be heard, "Come on, come on, keep going and don't look down, we're nearly there!" he called out as a fine mist rolled in reducing their visibility and soaked the children as they made their way along a very steep, slippery ledge.

Safely inside the shed, Baxter and Toby made their way outside into the garden and lay in the sunshine. "Let's take our clothes off down to our underwear and hang them on the branches of the tree. They should dry in this sunshine," suggested Beau. Inside the shed, they shivered as they began making plans for the following day. Then they heard their mother calling from outside the den.

"Come out immediately!" she demanded, the children reluctantly opened the door and went outside. Standing in their underwear they felt the warmth of the sun on their bodies, but they knew they were in big trouble. "Will somebody please tell me what on earth is going on here?"

"We've been playing with the water pipe and got our clothes wet," said Jay.

"Rubbish! Young man, don't you dare insult my intelligence," came a very sharp response. "If that's the truth, tell me why you didn't hang them on the clotheshorse? I'll tell you why!" their mother continued, "Because they're soaking wet, you've got mud all over them and didn't want me to see them, did you? Instead, you hung them on the tree and the dogs have had a field day jumping up and ripping your clothes to shreds.

"It's just not good enough and for that you're all going to spend the next week with me in the house and garden, doing some chores for a change, as a punishment."

Their mother continued, "You disappear for hours at a time and when you come back either your shoes are covered in mud or your clothes are wet through. I know you're up to something and it won't be long before I catch you out." Izabella was about to say something but stopped short when her mother gave her a very hard stare. "If anyone doesn't think it's fair, Izabella, I'll increase it from one week to two. You have to take responsibility for this silliness." Their mother wasn't very happy.

Chapter 18
Err on the Side of Caution

After giving it some thought, Paul decided to join the lads in the café the following day. Tom was the first to greet him. "Change of mind, mate?" said Tom.

"Well, you've given me a chance to do something that's really exciting, these things don't pop up every day and I felt I'd be letting you down if I didn't come."

"Come on, let's tell the others. If they don't like it, I won't go," said Tom.

"We're going to need you, so welcome back," said Billy. "Unfortunately the winds have increased so it's not safe to go today, we'll have to be patient and go when it's right. I've spoken to the Coast Guard, they reckon a high pressure is on its way so the sea should settle down in a day or two and the winds should drop. Of course there's no guarantee, anything can happen with the weather these days, but we need to err on the side of caution so I suggest we come back in two weeks' time. Let's meet in that café over there at 8:30, we'll grab a breakfast and look at the situation then." They all agreed.

Chapter 19
Daddy Loses His Job

Jane answered the phone. "Hello, sweetheart."

"Hello, I didn't expect your call at this time of day, is everything alright?"

"Bad news I'm afraid, unfortunately Mr Yardley, passed away this morning."

"Oh my goodness, that is bad news."

"The funeral's in two weeks' time, I feel I should stay for that."

"Yes of course."

"Jane, I've got more bad news which will affect us directly, best talk about that when I get back."

"Oh dear. No, tell me now please," said Jane.

"Are you sure you want to hear this over the phone?"

"Yes, it doesn't matter, what is it?"

"Well, they'd been planning to sell the business for years but because of Mr Yardley's age they decided to wait until he retired, apparently he's been ill for some time and kept it quiet. His children aren't interested in this type of business so they're going to sell it off immediately."

"What about his wife?" asked Jane.

"Apparently she died when she was very young and he never remarried."

"This is bad news."

"They've already sent out notices to the staff giving them a month's wage for every year and £500. The management will get two months' wages for every year plus £3,000 and a chance to buy the property that you happen to be living in at a reduced price. Those that can't afford to take up this offer will be given a chance to rent for 12 months, again at an agreed price. Then the properties must go on the market at the end of the year."

"This has been well planned, Stewart. It sounds like they're being fair and sympathetic to everyone."

"Yes love, that's what everybody's saying."

"Have they mentioned how much ours would be?" asked Jane.

"It's around £457,000."

"We haven't got that sort of money, so we'll be taking the renting option. But don't worry, Stewart, something good will come out of this, we will sort it out one way or another, I love you."

"I love you too," said Stewart.

"I won't mention it to the children, there's no need to upset them yet."

"Good idea, Jane. How are they doing?" asked Stewart.

Not wishing to burden Stewart with any more worries Jane simply said, "They're doing fine, no major problems."

"That's good to hear," said Stewart. "I'll give them a call tomorrow – I promise, bye for now, sweetheart."

"Bye," said Jane. As she replaced the phone she started to cry.

Overhearing the conversation and seeing her mother cry, Izabella quietly tip-toed out of the kitchen and ran back to the boys, crying uncontrollably. The children had been given the job of digging the garden as part of their punishment. Jay stood up as Izabella approached and asked what was wrong; Izabella was unable to speak at first. "You must tell us what's wrong, Izabella!" Jay demanded.

Wiping tears away with the back of the hand she took a deep breath. "I've heard Mummy talking to Daddy, we're going to have to move."

"Why?" Jay asked.

"I'm not going anywhere," said Beau.

Sobbing hard and fighting to catch her breath, Izabella continued, "Mummy's on her own and crying, somebody's died and Daddy's losing his job, we haven't got enough money for the house so we have to move."

Jay and Beau went very quiet, none of the children had seen or heard their mother cry before, it really unsettled them.

After a short while Jay told the others to stay where they were. "I'm going to see Mum."

Izabella put her hand on Jay's chest to stop him. "No, Jay I heard Mummy say she wouldn't tell us anything until Daddy comes home, they don't want to upset us."

"When's Daddy coming home?" asked Beau.

"I don't know," replied Izabella. Five minutes later Jane called them in for dinner. Hands washed they sat watching their mother's every move as she served dinner.

"You're all very quiet," said Jane, trying to a put on a brave face. "I've decided you've been punished enough, after dinner you can go out to play, just enjoy yourselves." The children didn't know how to react. "Hey come on you guys, your punishment is over, what's wrong?" asked Jane.

In tears, Jay told his mummy that Izabella had overheard her conversation with Daddy. Izabella started to cry.

"I didn't mean to, Mummy," she said. "I just came in to wash my hands and overheard you talking to Daddy. I saw you crying, Mummy."

Beau folded his arms on the table and buried his head hiding his tears.

"Hey come on my little team, it's all right, we'll sort something out, it's going to take some time but if you really want to make me happy, what I would like from you is to have as much fun as you can. I don't care if you get dirty or wet; just have fun and lots of it. But please, please be careful, that's all I ask."

The children didn't know whether to laugh or cry as they gathered round and gave their mummy the biggest cuddle ever.

The following week the children stayed out of the den and played in the garden with the dogs so they could keep a watchful eye on their mummy.

Jane felt tired as she made her way up the stairs to say goodnight to the children. "Have you brushed your teeth?" she asked.

"Yes we have," they replied.

"Why are you all in Jay's bed?" Jane asked.

"Jay's telling us one of Grandad's stories," Izabella said quietly.

"Alright, but when it's finished back to your own rooms please. By the way, I've not seen you in your den for over a week, is there anything wrong?" Jane enquired.

"We're thinking of going in tomorrow, Mummy, would that be OK?" asked Beau.

"Of course, just go and have some fun. I know you've been concerned for me and I do appreciate it, but I have lots to keep me busy and Daddy will be home soon. "

"When is he coming home?" Izabella asked.

"It won't be long now, sweetheart."

"Maybe he's just going to turn up and surprise us," said Jay.

"Sleep tight now, all of you." They wished their mummy goodnight and told her how much they loved her.

Chapter 20
Robin's Big Mistake

Billy, Robin, Tom and Paul sat in the beach café finishing off their breakfasts. "Robin, pass me one of the keys for the outboard engines, please," Billy asked, as he pulled what looked like a piece of plastic wire from his pocket. "I'm putting the key on this Kill Cord! Robin, do you know what to do with it?"

"It's the key for the rib!"

"Yes, but do you know how to use it?"

"I don't know what you mean," said Robin.

"Then let me explain. Whoever drives the rib needs to wrap this cord around their leg. See how it expands to fit any size? Then you put the key in the ignition and not before. If the driver went overboard with this around his leg it would pull the key out of the ignition and cut the engines. The rib would come to a standstill. I've heard of many accidents where people haven't used the Kill Cord and paid a heavy price."

"What happens?" asked Paul.

"Without using the Kill Cord, as you fall over board the key stays in the ignition and the rib continues on its own. After a while the rib begins the turn and goes round in circles, eventually it ends up heading straight for you! People think they can swim out of its way, but with less weight on board the rib is travelling much faster now and as it runs you over the propeller does the rest. You're dead!"

"I'll remember that," said Robin.

"You all remember that!" said Billy. "It's 8:15 a.m. now so we'll have that early start we planned, if everybody's ready, let's be on our way. I'll settle the bill," Billy told them.

At the counter the owner of the café asked, "Are you seriously going out to sea?"

"Yes," replied Billy, "we're quite used to this."

"Where you heading for?"

"Nowhere in particular, just doing a bit of sea fishing." Which of course wasn't the truth, but then Billy didn't want anyone knowing where they were heading for.

"Only the sea hasn't settled down yet, mate and there's a big tide on the way."

"Yes, we're aware of that, thank you," Billy replied. Blimey, this guy needs to know a lot, thought Billy. We've only had breakfast, can you imagine how many questions there'd be if we had a three-course meal?

The manager continued, "I'll make a note of the time you leave and how many people are in your rib."

"There is no need for that," said Billy. "We'll be alright."

"It's just so I can inform the Coast Guard if you don't get back at the time you give me, for your safety really, mate."

"I haven't got a time when we're coming back," Billy told him.

"Well, just your name then, you look like the leader."

That was the final straw! "OK mate, it's Captain Sensible."

"You're having a laugh," said the manager."

"No I'm not, " said Billy as he closed the door smiling and made his way over to join the others.

They'd been at sea for the best part of two hours. "I can see white horses out there," Paul shouted.

"What do you mean, 'white horses'?" asked Tom.

"It's water being blown off the tops of waves, look," said Paul pointing out to sea. "Can you see a fine white spray?"

"Yes I see what you mean," said Tom.

"Well, that's what people say, it looks like the white mane on the back of horses' necks, it's a good indication that the wind is picking up."

"You'll have to shout, I can't hear you," Robin said, shouting against the wind.

Paul repeated himself, "It's a good indication that the wind is picking up and the sea state is about to change, if it hasn't already done so."

"Are we safe out here?" Tom asked.

"Don't worry, this rib is quite capable of handling these conditions," Robin assured him.

"OK, but don't you think we should have the radios out and tuned into the right emergency frequency just in case we need help?" asked Paul.

"Alright lads, settle down," said Robin.

"Pass me the container with the radios and flares," asked Billy.

"I can't reach them, can somebody else move forward and get them please?" Robin shouted as he negotiated some large waves.

Paul moved forward, opening the storage locker. "They're not here!"

"Yes they are," said Robin. "In the blue container, not the white one."

"There's no blue container here!" Paul shouted back.

"Oh great!" Tom shouted. "Just a few things that could save our lives, and let me guess – you left them behind!"

Robin realized he'd left them in the boot of his car and in his defence he shouted back, "Well, did anyone else think to check before leaving shore? No, you left it all to me!"

"Only because you said you had it all covered," replied Paul.

"Look!" Billy shouted as the entrance to the cave came into view. "Slow down and lift the engines as the water gets shallow." Robin slowed the rib. "Nice one, now take her in gently," said Billy.

As they entered the cave the boys jumped into knee-deep water. Robin waited until Billy secured the rib before turning off the engines. "There's a lot of water here!" said Tom. But no one paid any attention to Tom's comments, nor did they question whether

Billy had misread the tide, instead they laughed and joked about the bumpy ride they'd had getting to the cave, all their fears had gone for now!

"Two and a half hours against that tide, not bad going," said Robin.

"Yeah, there was a few times I thought we were going to flip over! Perhaps you should have reduced your speed? Never mind, were here now," said Billy.

Robin took the Kill Cord from around his leg and joined the others, pulling the rib deeper into the cave. Unaware that one of the main bolts connecting engine number one, to the rib had cracked and was in danger of shearing off they continued.

"Look out for tree trunks," Paul shouted as he pushed one away from the side of the rib, allowing it to carry on its journey into the cave. As he did so he noticed the speed of the water. "This cave must be huge," he called out.

"What makes you say that," asked Robin.

"There's nothing coming back," Paul shouted. "Notice how the water's rushing forward, eventually you'd expect a bounce back."

"What do you mean by a bounce back?" asked Billy.

"It's what my dad called it, if the water doesn't show signs of bouncing back it a clear indication it's either going somewhere else or the cave's so deep it takes forever to hit the back of the cave. When it does the water bounces back a little."

"Well that's all very interesting, but which one is it?" Billy asked.

"Only time will tell," replied Paul.

By now they'd spent a long time in the cave and found nothing but floating debris. The rising water level went unnoticed. On a small ledge just below the water line something was shining, Tom rolled his sleeves up and placed one hand against the cave wall for support and bent forward trying to reach the object. As he lowered his other hand into the icy water, the depth surprised him as his chin touched the cold water, when his hand broke the surface he couldn't believe what he was looking at.

"Look!" he shouted. "A gold coin."

They all huddled round to take a look and gave a high-five. Still unaware of the increased depth and speed of water, they went deeper, searching eagerly now hoping to find more. Billy and Robin noticed what was left of a small wooden chest, inside a thin layer of sand acted as a temporary barrier protecting hundreds of gold coins.

"They're here, boys! We've found them, look!" they shouted.

By now the water level had reached their waist and Tom and Paul had difficulty trying to join the others to congratulate them. Robin lost his balance.

"Right, everybody settle down," Billy ordered. "This is how accidents happen, get these on the rib, there will be plenty of time for celebrations when we're back on dry land."

Robin looked at Tom. "I told you I'd keep my word, son."

"Yes you did, Dad." They smiled at each other for the first time in years.

"Be careful," said Billy, "we don't want to lose any."

Paul was the first to notice the rib floating away. "Robin, the rib!" he shouted.

In his excitement, Robin had let go of the rope they'd been using to pull the rib along, the strength of the incoming water knocked them off their feet as they tried to run after it. Tom was lucky, he saw an old tree trunk jammed between some rocks and held on to it with his right hand, at the same reaching out with his left to grab hold of Billy, saving him from being swept away. Paul and Robin had got swept against the rib and held on to its side.

Billy was frightened and started shouting out his orders. "It's time to get back in the rib and get out of here now!"

Nobody argued as they got back into in the rib, which had turned itself around after banging against some rocks and was now travelling backwards with the current. Tom and Paul managed to get in first then helped the others. Robin immediately went into his emergency procedures but forgot to put the Kill Cord around his leg. After making sure that everyone was sitting down he nominated Paul to be the lookout man.

"Tom," shouted Robin, "your job is to get rid of this water so start bailing out."

After doing so well he couldn't understand why the engines wouldn't start! All the time they were drifting backwards into a wall of fine mist, the sound of cascading water was overpowering. "Keep a look out for rocks!" Robin shouted. "I can't get the engines to start."

Looking back over Robin's shoulder Paul had noticed that most of the water was disappearing down a big hole!

"Robin!" He shouted. "Get those engines started now, come on!" Robin sensed the urgency in Paul's voice and looked up to see the terror in his eyes, Robin turned to face the danger.

"Come on, Dad!" Tom shouted.

Robin tried frantically but couldn't get them to fire up. "Keep trying!" Billy shouted.

Robin was running out of ideas, then for some unknown reason they burst into life. Thank God for that, Robin thought, but their troubles were far from over. Without warning the bolt that had cracked on their journey to the cave finally gave way and sheared off and engine number one, violently pulled itself of its housing, forcing the rib to turn sharply, the weight of the cage slid to one side throwing everyone into the ice-cold water, then engine number one collided with engine number two, the rib was now out of control.

If Robin had put the Kill Cord around his leg the engines would have stopped as he fell overboard, but he'd made that fatal mistake. Tom grabbed hold of a rope hanging from the rocks as he got swept along, Billy was trapped between the rib and the cave wall, Paul managed to climb up on some rocks while Robin hung onto the side of the rib. Again the engines collided with each other, the impact this time made the rib shoot forward slightly, freeing Billy; Robin was forced under water but came back up a few metres away clinging to jagged rocks.

Without radios or flares (it's fair to say that radios or flares wouldn't be much use to them inside the cave anyway), they were in great danger and the fact that Billy was reluctant to give the café owner information as to where they were heading for, left them completely isolated. It's considered being sensible when going out to sea to tell somebody where you're going and what time you're expected back, this could be a member of the family or the Coast Guard, it doesn't matter which. That way, if you get into difficulties at least somebody knows where about you're most likely to be. It could end up saving your lives!

Chapter 21
Heroes in the Making

After a good night's sleep and a hearty breakfast the children spent most of the day playing in the garden. By two o'clock in the afternoon the winds had strengthened and the temperature had dropped as black clouds engulfed the sky.

"Let's go in the den, it looks like rain," said Jay.

"I know," said Beau, "let's go visit our cave."

"Good idea," said Izabella.

Halfway down and the dogs sensed something was wrong but the children ignored their warnings and continued down. At the bottom of the steps just before the door they noticed the water was much deeper than usual, then a kind of roar sound came from the other side of the door leading into the cave. At first they thought they heard someone shouting but couldn't quite make it out with the dogs barking. Without taking their eyes off the door the dogs moved back and stood on the steps, barking more aggressively.

"Quiet! Quiet!" Jay shouted but the dogs continued.

"What's wrong with them" Beau asked.

"I don't know," said Jay. "Let's open the door."

"I don't think we should," said Bella.

"Why not?" Jay shouted.

"Something's wrong."

"There's nothing wrong, Bella," said Jay.

The boys pulled with all their strength until the door opened, luckily they managed to jump back just as the rib with its shark's white teeth shot by. Sparks lit the cave as the blades from the engines ripped across the rock face. The children stood there, totally shocked to see other people in their cave.

Paul shouted for help as he slid slowly back into the cold water next to Billy.

"Bella, you're the fastest runner, go and raise the alarm. Tell Mummy we need her help now," Jay ordered.

"Won't we get in to trouble?" asked Bella.

"No," said Jay, "these men are in danger and need our help now. Go!" he shouted, "and take the dogs with you."

Bella raced up the stairs with the dogs in close pursuit, through the shed, out in to the garden and straight into the house with her muddy boots still on. Finally she came to a stop in front of a policeman who was having a cup of tea with her mummy in the kitchen. She just stood there wide-eyed and open-mouthed.

"I certainly wouldn't want to be on the water today, there's a storm brewing, and the winds are getting stronger so I won't stay long. It's hard to pedal my bicycle when it's like this," said the officer as he pulled his notepad from his top pocket.

"I thought we were in for some good weather," said Jane.

"This wasn't forecast," he said. "They reckon the wind strength will reach gale force 10 before the day's out. With high tides it's going to get pretty bad out there, even the research vessel has come back into the docks seeking shelter. Apparently they've called off their search and are heading back to the USA – when they can. The weather is so unpredictable around these parts. But I've been told by a very reliable source that one of those top civil servants came from London to give them some bad news, but no one knows what that was all about."

Izabella was about interrupt.

"Oh yes," said the policeman, remembering why he'd made his visit. "I'm here, because there's been some criminal activity in the area over the last few months, so we're asking people to be aware and keep an eye out for that sort of thing. A rib has been reported stolen with its outboard engines but they won't get far with it. It's got big shark's teeth down both sides of it so it only a question of time."

Izabella's eyes almost popped out in disbelief. "Just shows their mentality really, I mean who would steal something like that?"

The dogs sensed that Bella wasn't going to interrupt the policemen, so they took off running through the country lanes to get Phil from the White House. A careless driver coming in the opposite direction clipped the back of Toby's leg and sent him flying into the bushes. Typically the driver hadn't realised he'd hit the dog and continued his journey. Baxter stopped, ran back and picked Toby up by the scruff of his neck and laid him gently on some soft grass before continuing to the White House.

In his garden, Phil was busy securing his garden furniture, which had been blown around by the strong winds. Baxter raced to his side wagging his tail and barking loudly, constantly looking back to the main gate. Phil knew Baxter was trying to tell him something and jumped into his Land Rover,. He opened the passenger door for Baxter to get in but Baxter wasn't having any of it, instead he ran off in front of the Land Rover until he reached Toby. Phil stopped and put Toby on the front seat, then Baxter jumped in and off they went. Thankfully Toby was just bruised a little and would soon be back on his feet.

As they pulled into the driveway at Hove-To, Stewart pulled in behind them; he'd just returned from Mr Yardley's funeral. "What's going on, Phil?" Stewart asked.

"I don't know, but your dogs are trying to tell me something, somebody might be in trouble."

Then they noticed the policeman's bicycle leaning against the hedge and rushed into the house. The police officer gave them a nod and continued reading from his white notebook, explaining that an old garage had been broken into and yellow life jackets, petrol cans, radios and emergency flares had all been reported missing.

"Just one moment please," Stewart interrupted. "Why are the dogs barking, Jane?"

"I have no idea," she replied.

"They're trying to tell you something, Daddy," said Izabella. "Some men are in danger, Daddy!"

"Which men, Izabella?"

"This is the first I've heard about this," said Jane. "Who's in trouble, sweetheart?"

They listened in disbelief as Izabella explained. At one point Jane was about to say something but stopped short when Izabella mentioned that Jay and Beau were trying to help.

"Where are they?" asked her daddy.

"In the big cave, Daddy."

"What big cave?" asked Stewart. "Show me, sweetheart."

Izabella, her daddy, Phil, and Baxter and Toby ran out of the house. The police officer, PC William Turner, had heard enough. From his short experience he knew when a child was telling the truth or not.

Speaking into his radio he asked to speak to the duty sergeant. "Hi young William, don't tell me you've caught some bank robbers?"

No Sarge, it's more important than that!"

"Go on, I'm listing, son," said Sergeant Spring as he took a sip of cold tea from his huge 'Best Grandad in the World' mug.

"We have a real emergency, Sarge."

"Do we now? I'll be the judge of that, young William."

"Four men and possibly two children are in danger in a cave just up from devil's mouth."

"Never heard of the place, lad."

"It's about four miles from the town heading southwest. I'm requesting immediate full emergency back up."

"What? You mean the lot?"

"Yes Sarge."

"Just hang on, lad. We've never done this before, where have you got this information?"

"From a young girl."

"You do realise, lad, that this is going to cost an awful lot of money and if you've got it wrong there will be consequences?"

"Sarge, her two brothers are in the cave now doing all they can to help, their father has just arrived home. Both he and a neighbour have gone to help."

"OK William, the call's gone out alerting the entire emergency services – the RNLI, the Coast Guard helicopter followed by Air Ambulance, the Fire Brigade, Coastal Watch, Paramedics, Police Helicopter, Experienced Climbers, Cave Rescue people and Rescue Dogs. Looks like my training worked well, young William. You've made the right call, well done lad. If this turns out well someone could end up with a commendation." For the briefest moment PC Turner thought he meant him, but then Sergeant Spring finished his sentence. "Do you know, lad, I've never achieved one of those before."

Helicopters raced across the dark sky as lifeboats spliced their way through rough seas, local inshore rescue boats made their way, hugging the coastline. Coastal watch manned their station as ambulances, fire engines and police cars raced down narrow lanes with their blue lights flashing and sirens sounding – all heading to this unfolding major incident. People ran along the cliff tops to offer local knowledge and help with hot drinks and sandwiches, and asked if anyone wanted a biscuit! Others came to sit and watch the drama unfold.

Izabella and the two dogs ran towards the secret den just as two maroons from the RNLI at Mevagesey shot into the blackened sky followed by two loud bangs! The explosions frightened Baxter and Toby so much they unexpectedly changed direction and tripped Izabella as they crossed her path. Falling, she hit her head and lay unconscious.

Dr Ward was already attending Izabella when Jane rushed to her side. "Carry on," she called out to Stewart.

"Hello, please allow me to introduce myself, I'm Dr Ward from the pink cottage. You're probably able to see it from your front bedrooms I would imagine."

"Yes, yes we can!" said Jane. "But this isn't the right time to be sociable is it?"

"No, of course not. Your daughter had a blow to the head." Oh really! State the obvious! Jane thought.

"She may have slight concussion for a while, you'll need to keep an eye on her, if you need me feel free to call at any time, it should last no more than a month or two and after that she should be back on her feet."

"Thank you, Dr Ward, you mentioned a slight concussion?"

"Yes, she's most likely to forget minor things but don't worry, everything will come back in time."

After laying Izabella on the sofa in the front room, Jane offered Dr Ward a cup of coffee.

Chapter 22
Life Jackets Save Lives

Inside the secret den the trapdoor had closed behind Izabella as she came out earlier. "This can't be what Izabella meant! There nothing here," said Stewart. Neither Stewart or Phil had noticed the outline of the trap door on the floor.

"Let's head for the cliff face," Stewart said. "Maybe they're down there." In driving rain they tried to find a way down. Then Phil noticed a rope in the under growth running over the cliff face.

"This must be what they've been using to get down."

"I doubt it, it's too dangerous, " said Stewart as he looked down. "But I can't rule it out."

They lowered themselves over the edge just as the winds increased, followed by a violent hailstorm.

"Just hang on!" Phil shouted as loud as he could. "This will pass soon."

The cliff face soon became slippery and unstable, Phil lost his footing and began sliding dangerously out of control until he hit a large rock protruding out of the cliff face, which saved him from a very nasty end.

They heard somebody using a megaphone. "YOU UP THERE, GO BACK, IT'S FAR TOO DANGEROUS FOR YOU TO COME DOWN, RETUN TO THE TOP IMMEDIATELY!"

Looking down through the driving hailstorm they were able to make out the letters RNLI on a rescue rib.

"Better do as they say," Stewart shouted, pointing to the top. They began their hard slippery climb back to the top. By now the Police and Coast Guard helicopters began to arrive. Television crews and newspaper reporters from all over the United Kingdom were racing through the country lanes trying to be the first to get this unbeliev-able story of missing children out to the world's television networks.

Using the rope they'd found in the toolbox, Beau quickly tied one end around a big rock, Jay shouted to Billy to hang on the other end, Billy made a grab for it but the power of the water began to pull him towards the big hole.

"Beau I've got an idea! Tie this rope around my waist, I'll make my way along the ledge, if I can fix this rope on those hooks over there we'll have a safety line."

"OK but be careful, it's really slippery along there!" Beau shouted, and then tapped Jay on the shoulder to indicate the job was done. Jay made his way along the ledge securing the line as he went, once he was convinced it was safe to do so he threw two lines down to Paul and Billy.

"Wrap them around your waist!" Jay shouted, Paul managed to get his on, but Billy was having trouble and Paul hadn't the strength to help.

"Hold on to the ropes, Jay. Pull them out when I'm ready!" shouted Beau as he launched himself off the ledge into the cold water. He told Billy what he was about to do: "I'll wrap this around your waist, just hang on." Then he shouted back to Jay to start pulling. Billy was exhausted but tried to do what he could to help. Once out of the water Billy felt safe sitting next to Jay.

Paul was next; being younger he found it a lot easier but still needed a little help from Beau. On the other side Robin shouted for help, the cold water was taking the heat from his body and his fingertips had already turned blue. In a desperate attempt to save himself he made a grab for a rope hanging from the back of the speeding rib as it shot by. This dragged him under the water but thanks to his life jacket it brought him back to the surface, then he disappeared again.

Jay and Beau stood shouting, "Let go of the rope!" But when he came up for the third time they realised his hand had got entangled in the rope and he couldn't let go. Without thinking, Paul dived in, without a life jacket on, in a brave but dangerous attempt to save

Robin. But the rib was travelling so fast it left Paul in the water and he began to drift deeper in to the cave. Almost out of sight of the others he managed to swim to the edge and climbed out exhausted. Unable to help he sat there waiting to be rescued. The boys watched as the rib charged out of control deeper into the cave taking Robin with it.

Izabella lay on the sofa recovering from her accident, although she felt unsteady on her feet and a little sick she made her way to the patio doors. She was surprised to see so many people, what was a helicopter doing hovering over the top of her house! And why had one landed at the top of the garden! How strange, she thought.

Then it all came racing back, filling her head with all sorts of things. She began to feel sick and dizzy but took flight, running past a man standing in the garden.

"What are you all doing here and who are you?" she shouted.

"I'm Tony Brewster," he said. "The helicopter pilot, and who might you be?"

"Izabella Redgrave! Where's my Daddy?" she demanded.

"On the coastal path looking for your brothers I think!"

Then it all came back to her.

"Well tell him he's looking in the wrong place!" Izabella shouted as she entered the den.

Jane had finished her coffee. "I'll just go and see how my princess is doing," she told the doctor.

"I'll come with you, she should be feeling better having had a rest."

They entered the lounge to find the patio doors wide open and no sign of Izabella. Running into the garden they came across Tony Brewster, the helicopter pilot. Have you seen a little girl?" Jane demanded.

"Yes she's just gone in there," he said pointing to the den. "She's trying to find her father, apparently he's looking in the wrong place."

Jane asked the doctor to find her husband while she went into the den, hoping to find Izabella. Jane noticed the opening to the passage way and came back out shouting for a torch – just as Stewart, Phil the police officer and a paramedic came running down from the coastal path.

"Inside the den," Jane shouted. "They're down there." Izabella had pushed the trap door so far back the hinges had snapped off and the door stayed open. Thankfully the police and paramedic carry torches so Pedro the paramedic offered his torch to Stewart as they entered the passageway.

Izabella was well ahead of them by this time. Entering the cave she noticed a body floating face down in the water, quickly she put on her lifejacket, dived in and swam at speed towards it. Once she reached the body she immediately turned it over on to its back, Robin gasped for air.

A moment or two longer and Robin would have drowned. Supporting him with one arm to keep his face out of the water she forced her left hand into a gap in the rocks and clenched her fist to make a wedge, this stopped them from being pulled towards the big hole. All she could do now was hope it wouldn't be too long before someone came to their rescue.

Tom sat on a rock just above the water, exhausted and unaware that the rib had chosen its next victim and was heading straight for him. With seconds to spare Tom realised the danger and dived as deep as possible, hoping to avoid the spinning blades. They passed over his feet by a few centimetres leaving a trail of air bubbles as the engine shot by. When he resurfaced he came up next to Izabella and Robin, he was surprised but glad to see that such a young girl had come to their rescue.

Jay and Beau carefully made their way along the ledge with more ropes, trying to get close enough to throw a line to Izabella. Jay lost his balance and slipped, hitting his head on the rocks below and entered the cold water.

"Are you alright, Jay!" Beau shouted.

"Yes it's not too bad, I'll be alright." He hadn't noticed the blood running down his face and swam over to Tom. As he got closer he was sure he saw someone holding onto the rocks, for a moment he thought it was another member of the group in trouble.

"Bella!" he called out. "What are you doing here? Where's Mum and our help?"

As he took Robin's hand Jay realized Izabella too had come to their rescue. "I'll explain later, Jay, but help is on the way," said Izabella.

Jay took control. "Tom, tie this rope around his waist and keep him on his back at all times. Bella and I'll help by pushing him along while Beau pulls us all over. But first we'll tie ourselves together until we're out of danger. The current is getting really strong now we don't want anyone being swept away."

They made a slow but steady progress. Beau used all his strength pulling against the currents they were less than four metres from the edge.

Billy stood up; he'd been watching the whole event from the side and was sure he heard something; straining his eyes he looked deep into the cave. He listened for that sound again. This time he knew he was right. "It's the rib!" he shouted. "The rib's coming! Get out!"

"Where is it?" Jay called.

"I can't see yet but I can hear it."

"It's coming back, swim faster!" Billy shouted.

They looked around but were unable to see it. It was impossible to locate the rib as it hid behind the wall of mist, but now they too could hear it smashing against the rocks as it made its way towards them.

"Come on, son!" Billy shouted. Then Jay caught a glimpse of it as it punched through the thick mist, its painted teeth reminding him of a big white shark searching for its next prey.

"Swim faster it's coming!" Jay called.

But it was too late, the rib went between them splicing the ropes before running out of fuel.

Tom began drifting towards the big hole, tired and without a life jacket he was in great danger. Jay, Izabella and Beau managed to get Robin safely to the side. The children by this time were exhausted and began to look for a way out just as their father and Big Phil entered the cave. Bella had done her job and at long last help had arrived!

Stewart and Phil made their way slowly along the ridge and realised just how challenging it must have been for the children. They helped take Robin up to the doorway where the paramedics were waiting. Jay, Izabella and Beau were all in need of medical attention; the medics wrapped them in space blankets and attended to Jay's head and Beau's rope burns on his hands. Izabella had swam at great speed to save Robin and needed to rest.

"Look! The rib's stuck on the edge of the hole," said Izabella. "There's someone in the water." She was about to jump in when her father grabbed her arm.

Paul could see his mate Tom drifting towards the hole and entered the water again in an attempt to help him. But soon found himself in trouble, drifting towards the hole with the ropes that Jay and Beau had tied around their waist trailing behind him.

Big Phil was already in the water trying to reach the trailing ropes. Tom shouted to Paul, "I'm sorry, mate! It was never meant to be like this."

There was no reply as they went over the edge. Big Phil had managed to grab hold of their ropes and stood inside the rib using it as a platform. Hoping it would stay in place, he waited until all the slack had been taken up on their lines. Then Phil pulled with all his strength to stop the boys from falling any further, his arms were shaking under the strain now and he knew couldn't hang on much longer.

Tom looked up and recognised the big man but couldn't remember where from. "I can't hold you both forever!" Phil shouted. "Start making a move."

"Let me go if you have to!" Paul shouted.

"No, let me go, this is my fault," said Tom.

All the emergency services were now in the cave ready to offer help, but all they could do was watch the events unfold. They knew if anyone made the slightest move and broke Phil's concentration all three could lose their lives.

"Come on!" Phil shouted. As he looked down he could see both lads trying to undo the rope around their waists, each one trying to break free so the other would survive. Phil realised what was going on and gave out an almighty ear-piercing cry that echoed around the cave. He lifted both boys at the same time from the water and on to the rib. Everyone cheered as the RNLI inshore rescue team raced to pick them up. When everyone was safely on board, the RNLI pulled away. There was a loud groan as the rib turned showing its teeth for the very last time before it disappeared down the hole on its way to who knows where.

Chapter 23
Time to Face the Truth

One by one everybody made their way back through the passageway, up the steps and through the shed out into the back garden. A reporter approached Stewart. "Do you mind if I ask you a few questions, sir? Are these courageous children yours?"

"Yes they are and we're very proud of them," said Stewart.

"I've heard a lot of gold coins have been found? I'm wondering who will be claiming the reward?"

Before Stewart answered, Billy interrupted. "I'll tell you who, the children that's who, they saved our lives and without them none of us would be alive today, they'll get the reward – all of it," said Billy.

"The police informed me that the rib and a few other things are stolen property. Now, if that's the case do you know who stole them?" asked the reporter.

"That's police business," said Stewart. "They will deal with that, what I can say is that my family had nothing to do with any stolen property. On the question of the reward, I would like to thank Billy for his kind offer but let's find the true value of these coins and talk about it then."

"When will you be able to retrieve the gold coins?" the reporter asked.

"Probably later this evening when the tide's out, it will be a lot safer then."

"Are the police preventing people from entering the cave?"

"Yes, I believe so."

"What will happen to…?"

But before the reporter could ask his question, Stewart interrupted.

"You'll have to excuse me. I believe the police are waiting for an interview."

On his way to the police, Jane called Stewart. "This is Dr Ward from the pink cottage."

"Hello Doctor."

"Good afternoon, Mr Redgrave, your children are doing remarkably well considering what they've been through. Izabella will suffer with a slight concussion for a few months."

"How bad is it?"

"Very slight, you'll have to be patient, she won't be able to remember names or places for a while and probably won't remember where she's put things, but that should come back as I say in a few months' time. If that's not the case I would like you to call me immediately."

Stewart thanked the doctor and made his way to the police officer.

Tom sat drinking a cup of tea as Phil approached. "I know you don't I?" said Phil. "You're the young lad who came off worst in the café a few months ago."

"Yeah that's me," said Tom.

"I recognise you now."

"I went back to the café hoping to find you and apologise for my behaviour. Look, this may not be the right time or place but I do apologise." Phil offered his hand as token of friendship and Tom accepted it and thanked him for saving their lives.

"Can I ask? Where did you get the strength from to pull us both out like that?"

"I don't know," said Phil. "What I do know is that I had no intention of letting you go. When this is over give me a call, I'd like to get to know you better."

"I'll do that," said Tom.

PC Tuner called the boys together. "Right lads, there's a question of stolen property, does that involve everybody?"

"No it doesn't," Robin said. "They didn't know anything about it."

"Why did you do this, Dad?" Tom asked.

"In my own stupid way, son, I hoped this adventure would have brought us closer together and for that I was willing to risk everything. I know I've blown it, son."

"No you haven't," said Tom. "Money isn't everything, I'll come with you to the police station as your son and friend, our bond is stronger than we both thought, Dad."

Phil and Stewart stood by listening. "Officer," Phil interrupted. "We know who this gear belongs to!"

"Who might that be?" asked the policeman.

"Everything apart from the rib belongs to a cousin of mine and he won't be pressing charges, I'll see to that," said Phil. "As for the rib, well that belongs to Charlie Henshaw! You'll know his track record so he won't be pressing charges, will he? We can have all the gear back to its rightful owner in a couple of hours if it's OK with you."

The officer thought for a while and realised it would save him a lot of paperwork. "Alright," he said, and with his very best firm voice added, "Make sure it's done. You're a very lucky man," he said looking at Robin. "If I ever hear you're involved in anything like this again you'll be locked up, do you understand?" said the police officer.

"I do," said Robin. "Right then our job's done," said the police officer as he jumped into the helicopter.

Chapter 24
Everything isn't What it Seems

Two months later the autumn equinox had arrived on the 21st of September and with it came a cold wind from the east. Stewart had finished his job at the forestry and the family were in the process of moving out. Although the house was offered to them they knew they couldn't afford it. Sitting at the dining room table Stewart watched the children play in the autumn's sunshine. The phone rang. Jane answered. "It's for you, sweetheart. A Mr Arkwright." Stewart walked through into the hallway,

Arkwright? Who's Arkwright, he thought. "Stewart Redgrave here, how can I help?"

"Hello Mr Redgrave, Charles Arkwright here from the Ministry of Treasures and Valuation, we need to meet and discuss your recent find."

"Yes, I began wonder whether you were interested or not. When I rang your office yesterday they said they would be in touch in a few weeks."

"That's probably a misunderstanding by our junior clerks. I can only apologise, but of course we're interested. I will be dealing with this from now on so you won't need to ring the office in future. Now you're more than welcome to come to my office or I'll visit your home, which I believe would be more convenient for you all. I realise you'll need to gather all the people involved. Would you please inform them they will be breaking the law if they don't attend the meeting? Failing to do so could lead to prosecution, which may well lead to a spell in prison. I'll give you one week then, Mr Redgrave, if that's OK with you? I hate to put pressure on you like this but I'm afraid that's how government works on matters of this nature. They simply like to get things in order, sorted quickly so to speak."

Stewart hadn't time to think. "Yes, yes err, at mine in one week's time that's fine, fine, thank you, Mr Arkwright." He ended the call.

One week later everybody gathered in the Redgrave's sitting room. "Well, this is quite a gathering," said Mr Arkwright. "I'll get straight to the point, I'm afraid to inform you that the coins that you found are all fakes. We believe that when the square-rigger Destiny did battle with the Spanish fleet she fell for the oldest trick in the book. The Spanish were renowned for carrying fake coins and often removed the floorboards below decks to stash the real treasure deep inside the guts of the ship. After replacing the floorboards they'd stack fake gold on the top decks and cover them with old sails and empty barrels to make out they were hiding something of value in case they were attacked. Now unfortunately for you good people who have risked life and limb, you've achieved nothing. Except perhaps true friendships, I suppose! Some would say that's worth more than money. Before anyone asks about the find on the American survey vessel Wild-Thing, they too had the same bad news."

"So that's why they were ready to pull out as the storm arrived," Paul said. "Quite right," said Mr Arkwright. Izabella asked if she could be excused to help mummy make tea. No one had anything to say as they sat thinking of all the risks they'd taken.

Mr Arkwright continued. "The Ministry had hoped that this might have been the treasure chest the world has been waiting for, by that I mean for many years we've all been looking for a single coin they call the Secret Coin, very much like the ones you found, it has a warrior with a spear on one side and a child's face on the other, but around its edge it has the words Protector of Honesty. The coin is believed to be one of the oldest in the world and some say it has magical powers. Even today it's almost impossible to put a price on it. The whole world is searching for it now and we know one day it will show up."

"Well I can tell you no one here has come across anything like that, have we lad?" said Stewart.

"I'm willing, that is the Crown is willing, to pay each and everyone the sum of £100."

Izabella returned to the room unaware of what Mr Arkwright had just said about a secret coin.

"Then you'll sign a paper legally preventing you from talking or writing about your find, or the amount you're about to receive for being involved in the find."

"That's crazy, why the need to keep it quiet?" asked Billy.

"I'm afraid I'm bound by the laws of this country not to discuss this matter any further, before we continue I must ask you if you're in agreement or not."

"Does this mean we can't sell our stories to the newspapers or television?" Tom asked.

"I'm afraid it does," said Mr Arkwright.

"Does that include the children?" asked Stewart.

"Yes I'm afraid it does. Little ones soon become adults, don't they? So they must sign the contract.

"What would happen if one of us informed say a television company?" Robin enquired.

Arkwright gave Robin a hard stare. "Imprisonment. Without a doubt," he said.

One at a time they reluctantly agreed to sign. "Thank you," said Mr Arkwright. "Now I have everyone's signature I must be on my way."

"What about our money?" Billy asked.

"The money will be paid directly into your bank accounts, the children's money will go into the parents' account and they will have to sort it out from there."

"How do you know our bank accounts?" Tom asked.

"Your government knows everything about you, young man," replied Mr Arkwright.

Stewart walked Mr Arkwright to the garage at the side of the house and helped his chauffeur load all the fake coins into the boot of his limousine. "What will happen to all of this now?" Stewart asked.

"Off to the mint I'm afraid, to be melted down back to base metal, that's all its worth."

"I certainly wouldn't like your job, Mr Arkwright."

"Why's that?"

"Well, it must be difficult going around the country telling people what they thought was a life changing opportunity had come to nothing. However, I thank you for your time, Mr Arkwright."

"Yes you're right, it is hard, I don't make the rules just follow them, you have three remarkable children, look after them, Mr Redgrave."

"Thank you, I will."

The chauffeur closed the passenger door. Mr Arkwright smiled then nodded to the chauffeur and the black limousine quietly pulled away.

"Has it been successful, sir?" the driver asked.

"Of course," replied Arkwright. "So you can put that away! The driver pressed a button on the dashboard and placed the gun inside the hidden compartment. "The gold's ours."

"Any news on the secret coin, sir?"

"No, it's not there! So they say, but we won't be too far away just in case."

"You seem a bit upset, sir."

"Well, he happens to be a nice guy and has a lovely family, sometimes even in this business you have a conscience."

Chapter 25
A Crushing Blow

Mr Arkwright had left Stewart his mobile number but after several failed attempts, Stewart decided to ring the main office of Treasure and Valuation. "We haven't anyone by the name of Arkwright on our books, sir. It's highly unlikely that any government officials from here would arrange such a meeting. This type of arrangement would go against the government's policies, sir. You would have been invited to the Treasure and Valuation office to discuss your find, sir."

Stewart felt a sickness in his tummy. It wasn't fool's gold after all. Arkwright had taken away the real thing, we're the only fools! he thought.

At the local police station the Chief Inspector asked, "Has anyone got any correspondence or any other evidence?"

Stewart shook his head and said, "No."

"Did anyone take the registration number of the limousine?"

"This is going to sound really stupid but I don't think so," said Stewart.

"In that case, sir," said the Chief Inspector, "with no leads, there's not much we can do."

Stewart arranged a meeting at his home and informed everyone of the bad news. "If anybody tried to sell the story to the press you're going to look pretty foolish, remember," he said. "Arkwright got us all to sign those papers! None of us really understood what we were signing for, we've been well and truly stitched up." The joy and excitement came to a crushing blow as the thought of not getting anything sunk in. "If anyone doubts what I'm saying is true, you're more than welcome to ring this number," said Stewart.

"No one doubts you, Stewart," said Billy.

Chapter 26
A Very Special Home

A few days later the family continued packing boxes ready for the move. "Stewart," Jane called, "Would you mind taking these bins out before someone trips over them please?" In his rush to get back in the warmth he hadn't noticed that one of the bags had a split down the side which burst open before he got anywhere near the bins. The wind scattered the rubbish all over the garden and Stewart could be seen running after it like a mad man. He reached the top of his drive just as a taxi arrived. Who could this be? he thought. The taxi continued down the drive and Stewart followed.

The driver got out and opened a rear passenger door to assist an elderly lady to her feet. "Good afternoon, Stewart. Oh don't look so surprised, would you mind if we get out of this cold wind. I'll see you back here in two hours, young man," she instructed the taxi driver.

"Yes madam."

"I shall settle my bill then, off you go," said the elderly lady. As she entered the hallway she felt the warmth.

"Ahh that's better. Stewart, it's nice to be back!"

Back? Stewart thought, then called Jane to come and meet Mrs Brody, Mr Yardley's, secretary. At first both Jane and Stewart felt uncomfortable, why on earth had this woman – who couldn't even congratulate Stewart when he became a senior manager and was so rude to him at the time – bother to call?

"Would you like a cup of tea, Mrs Brody?" Jane asked.

"Yes that would be nice, but please call me Viv and just a little milk thank you and no sugar. Where are the children, Stewart?" she asked.

"Still at school."

"Yes, of course, how silly of me."

Jane returned with the best china. "Would you like a sandwich?" Jane asked.

"No thank you, I'm fine."

"A biscuit?"

"Shall we get on?" said Mrs Brody. "Now you must be wondering why I'm here but first, Stewart, I have to apologise to you for my behaviour when you came for your job interview."

"Oh that's alright, Mrs Brody, I mean Viv, there no need to apologise."

"Well I disagree, I should explain that at the time of your interview Mr Yardley was seriously ill and refused to let anybody know, obviously we knew you were coming and he asked me to deal with you as quickly as possible and if I had to be rude to you, so be it. He didn't want anybody to see him suffer you see."

Stewart was about to say something.

"No please let me finish," said Mrs Brody. Jane reached out and touched Stewart's hand as a comforting gesture to let her carry on. "He was really pleased to see you apply for the post. You wouldn't have known but Mr Yardley had an eye on you right from the start and knew one day you would be sitting right here in this very house."

"How could he have known that?" asked Stewart.

Viv continued without any explanation. "It's a house where Mr Yardley and my family spent lots of time together. This is a very special home full of wonderful surprises, Stewart, and that's what's brought me here today."

Both Jane and Stewart looked at each other slightly puzzled.

Viv continued. "When I was a young girl, at the tender age of eighteen I began working for Mr Yardley. He was about twenty-three I think. He knew then where he was going in life and how things would turn out. I remember my first encounter with his solicitor, I was asked to sign two letters, which I duly did. The solicitor offered to keep them in a safe place, but Mr Yardley said that wouldn't be necessary, 'this young lady,' he said pointing at me, 'will be my secretary for many years to come and I know I'll have her total trust to look after things like that'. Now, how he knew I'd be his secretary for the next fifty-seven years was beyond me. But that's exactly what happened. After his death I was left with all the legal papers to deal with and the responsibility of clearing out the offices. The last thing to be moved was the famous whiskey cabinet."

"I remember that," said Stewart. "Whiskey from around the world!"

"That's right, and behind it the removal man discovered these two envelopes, you can see there's no address on them so I opened them both and instantly recognised them to be the two letters that I signed many years ago. I never knew what had happened to these until yesterday. I knew they were left on top of the cabinet and that was the last time anyone saw them and to my knowledge no one ever mentioned them again. I can only assume they must have slipped behind the cabinet after the meeting and that's where they stayed. I'll read this one and then I'd like you to read the second, Stewart, if that's alright."

"Yes of course," said Stewart.

"I, Mr Gordon Yardley on this day the 1st of August 1957, agree to pay the sum of £3000 as an extra bonus for each year's loyal service to my secretary Mrs Viv Brody and I expect the sum to be in excess of £171,000 by the time of my death. This must be settled before any member of my family takes any inheritance."

"I don't know what to say," said Stewart. "How on earth did he know all that?"

"We'll never know, Stewart," said Mrs Brody as she passed the second letter and asked him to read it out loud. Stewart gave a gentle cough to clear his throat before he continued.

"To whom it may concern, I Mr Gordon Yardley on this day the 1st of August 1957, give notice to the person in residency at Hove-To at the time of my death shall inherit the property…"

"What!" Stewart shouted in disbelief.

"Please carry on, Stewart," asked Mrs Brody.

"…and all its surroundings." Stewart could hardly breathe, his eyes filled with tears of joy.

"Please go on, Stewart," asked Mrs Brody.

"As a sign of gratitude for his hard work and loyal service." Both Jane and Stewart were overcome.

"This is unbelievable, things like this just don't happen to us," said Jane.

"Do read on please, Stewart," said Mrs Brody, just as the taxi, sounded its horn. "Ahh my taxi has arrived," said Mrs Brody as she got to her feet. "Well, I don't suppose we'll meet again but I wish you all the luck for the future, good day to you both." It was as if she hadn't been there at all, in no time she'd gone and the house felt strangely empty. Stewart and Jane were left standing in the hallway.

"Is this a miracle?" said Jane, I can't wait to tell the children."

"Why me?" Stewart asked.

"Pardon?" said Jane with a slight frown across her forehead.

"Why did he have a watchful eye on me?"

"Sweetheart, it doesn't matter, don't worry about it now. Our home is safe that's fantastic news isn't it?"

"Yes I realise that but something is bothering me."

"Remember Mrs Brody asked you to read on just as her taxi arrived? Finish reading the letter, Stewart."

"This house has fond memories and will look after you and your family, good luck, Stewart – Stewart! How did he...?"

"Please read on, Stewart," said Jane.

"Your family will find the treasures one day." Steward gasped. "Don't you see? How did he know someone by the name of Stewart would be here, and that link to treasure, what does it all mean?"

"I don't know, I don't understand but you're beginning to make me nervous," said Jane.

"Make you nervous? How do you think I feel? There has to be an explanation! But where do we find it?"

"Push the front door to, Stewart, it's come open by itself again."

"Why does it do that?"

"I've no idea."

"I'll put the kettle on," said Jane. "Let's settle down and to try to make some sense out of this before the children come home."

Chapter 27
Who's Mr Redgrave?

On his way to the kitchen the phone rang.

"Pick it up, Stewart."

"Hello, the Redgrave's residence."

"Mr Gravies here, the children's headmaster. Unfortunately Izabella's met with an accident in the school playground and is now on her way to hospital."

"How bad is it?"

"Not sure, but she had a nasty injury to her head, her brothers were close by when this happened so I've sent them along as they seem to be the only ones who can make any sense out of what she's saying. I thought it best, until one of her parents arrive. I suggest you make your way to the hospital."

"Yes of course thank you, Mr Gravies."

Driving through heavy traffic they arrived some forty minutes later, the nurse on reception looked a little concerned as she directed them to the end cubicle, half-way down the ward the duty doctor called them back.

"Excuse me! Who did you say you were?"

"The parents of Izabella Redgrave."

"Well that's strange."

"What's strange?" asked Stewart.

"I've already had a Mr Redgrave here!" Jay overheard his father and came from behind the curtain that the nurse had pulled around Izabella's bedside.

"Dad, Mr Arkwright's been here, asking lots of questions about the secret coin."

Holding her head on both sides Izabella shouted, "Daddy, I haven't told him anything!"

Stewart and Jane looked puzzled, the doctor asked if he could be of any help.

"Yes, call the police. My daughter might be in danger."

The doctor instructed the receptionist to call the police immediately and then went to check on Izabella. She began to tell her parents about the secret coin.

Stewart interrupted, "Izabella sweetheart, we'll talk about this later, now you need to rest."

The doctor examined Izabella for the second time. "Well, Izabella, after your examination I'm happy to say your condition has improved and if it remains stable you should be home tomorrow, I think it's best you stay overnight so we can keep a check on you." The doctor's pager went off. "I'm afraid I have to go; I'll try and catch up with you in the morning." The doctor left the cubicle.

"Well that's good news, sweetheart. At least you'll be home tomorrow," said Jane.

"Daddy, Jay and Beau have told me all about the secret coin and the magic powers it might have and how valuable it is. I remember now that when Mr Arkwright came to our house I'd left the room to help Mummy make tea for everyone, so I didn't know anything about the coin. But I do remember having a nasty dream about a pirate ship and me sinking to the bottom of the sea. Daddy, I found that coin when we first went down the cave and put it in my pocket, I'd forgotten all about it until you told us about having to pay a bounty on things you found. I got frightened and thought we might all get into trouble, so I put it in one of my jewellery cases and threw it out my bedroom window, it must still be there, Daddy, in Mummy's flower beds under my window somewhere."

They heard the police arrive at reception. Stewart popped his head out from behind the curtain and was pleased to see that PC William Turner had been made a sergeant for his quick thinking in an emergency situation. Stewart brought him up to date about Mr Arkwright's visit and agreed to have a police officer standing outside Izabella's cubicle overnight, just in case Mr Arkwright retuned. With the help of the receptionist arrangements had been made for Jane, Jay and Beau to stay overnight. Stewart insisted he would stay at Izabella's bedside.

Chapter 28
The Children's Generosity

Three months later Billy, Robin, Tom, Paul and Phil, together with the official Treasury Department, were invited to the Redgrave home. Stewart cleared his throat. "First let me say how nice it is to see you all. Where to start!" said Stewart. "Well, you're all aware of the secret coin from that no good for nothing Mr Arkwright and that's why we're here today, you see that part of his story is true. What you don't know is that the coin has been found." Everyone spoke at once.

"For the safety of the children," Stewart continued, "Only the Treasury Department were aware of the find, that's why they're here today. We've had to keep it quiet until we were ready to tell the world, but before we do we wanted you to know."

"Well good for you," Billy shouted.

"Thank you, Billy. The children wanted to let you know what they intend to do with the reward. But first I have to tell you that Mr Arkwright is hanging around and has made contact with the children, how he knew that Izabella was admitted to hospital concerns us, the police are trying to track him down but have very little to go on at the moment, so I ask you all to be aware and stay alert. If you do see him contact the police. The children have decided that the British Museum is the safest place for the coin."

"That's very commendable," said Tom, "but surely the children are entitled to a reward?"

"I'm glad you've mentioned the reward, Tom. There has been a settlement and you'll be told how much shortly by the Official Treasury Department. But first let me tell you the wishes of the children, they have decided that it's to be shared with all of you, and donations are to be made to the RNLI the Police and Coastal Helicopter fund, the paramedics and the dog rescue service. The Treasury will ask you to sign papers preventing you from disclosing how much each person has received, and this time, lads, they're genuine. This is for the safety of all of us."

The man from the Treasury handed out the papers, once signed he gave everyone a cheque and thanked them for their generosity on behalf of all the Emergency services.

By the time everyone had gone it was late and time for bed, Stewart put the three children in one bedroom until things settle down. Jane and Stewart wished them a goodnight. "You've had a busy time, sleep well now," said Jane as she closed the bedroom door; they overheard the children say how they wished Grandad was there to tell them a bedtime story.

"Grandad's never far away," Stewart whispered.

THE END

Granddad's stories
Glossary

Nudge	A light touch or push.
Correction Centre	A place for young persons that have committed crimes before
CCTV	Closed circuit television
Remission	Early release
What's your grass brother	Slang for what do you want.
Inheritance	Money or objects that are passed on to members of the family
Con	A scam or confidence trick
Road Crew	Men that repair the roads
Dole	Payment you receive from the government if you're out of work
Per Annua	Means every year, Yearly
RNLI	Royal National lifeboat institution
Krill	A fishing box to put fishing equipment in.
Kosher	Slang for something that's genuine and legitimate
Baccy	Is what pirates used to call tobacco
Retirement	A time when you've reached the age to finish work
White-collar workers	People who generally work in offices
Montepulciano	A red wine from Eastern Central Italy

Salary and Bonuses	Salary is your wage, Bonus a reward for working harder
Receipts	A written record of what you have paid for.
Prevailing winds	Blows at a particular time
Bounty	What pirates stole from ships?
Shondablur	A word made up by granddad, which can mean anything!
Survey Ship	A research vessel designed and equipped to carry out research at sea
Pontoon	A temporary bridge or a floating landing stage mostly found in docks
The Lookout Man	Keeps an eye out for obstacles both on top and under the water
Bail	Using a bucket to get rid of water from inside a Rib or Boat
Maroon	Rockets fired by RNLI to call crewmembers to the station
Commendation	An award or honour, for doing something honourable
Diss	Slang for 'this'
Readies	Slang for money
Captain Sensible?	No not really. It's considered being sensible when going out to sea to tell somebody where you're going and what time you're expected back, this could be a member of the family or the Coast Guard it doesn't matter which. That way, if you get into difficulties at sea at least somebody knows where about you're most likely to be. (It could end up saving your lives!)